ONE PIECE AT A TIME

Ian Yates

Text Copyright © 2013 Ian Yates

All rights reserved

No unauthorised reproduction whether it be electronic or manual and no unauthorised digital transmission is allowed in accordance with copyright law.

CONTENTS

ACKNOWLEDGEMENTS 7

CHAPTER 1 11

CHAPTER 2 13

CHAPTER 3 19

CHAPTER 4 23

CHAPTER 5 27

CHAPTER 6 29

CHAPTER 7 33

CHAPTER 8 38

CHAPTER 9 42

CHAPTER 10 48

CHAPTER 11 50

CHAPTER 12 57

CHAPTER 13 59

CHAPTER 14 65

CHAPTER 15 69

- CHAPTER 16 73
- CHAPTER 17 78
- CHAPTER 18 84
- CHAPTER 19 88
- CHAPTER 20 91
- CHAPTER 21 95
- CHAPTER 22 101
- CHAPTER 23 104
- CHAPTER 24 109
- CHAPTER 25 113
- CHAPTER 26 121
- CHAPTER 27 124
- CHAPTER 28 130
- CHAPTER 29 133
- CHAPTER 30 138
- CHAPTER 31 144
- CHAPTER 32 149

CHAPTER 33 154

CHAPTER 34 159

CHAPTER 35 162

CHAPTER 36 170

CHAPTER 37 175

CHAPTER 38 180

CHAPTER 39 185

CHAPTER 40 191

CHAPTER 41 198

CHAPTER 42 204

CHAPTER 43 209

CHAPTER 44 217

CHAPTER 45 221

CHAPTER 46 226

ONE PIECE AT A TIME

Acknowledgements

To everyone whose name I have used and changed slightly (sometimes), I thank you for allowing me to create characters around you…even when those characters may be nothing like you in real life and especially when they are.
I thank you all. (And no…there will be no royalty cheque in the post Mrs. C)

Eric, the master proofreader, your assistance was amazing. If it wasn't for you, my work would have been full of errors that I was blissfully unaware of

For my Mum, a big thank you for everything and I hope you don't mind the promotion to Superintendent from your original rank in the Police force.

To Helen, a true fighter who gave me the inspiration for the strong character in this story.

And for Alison, my wife. I cannot put into words the love I feel for your encouragement and patience when I first spoke about writing this novel. Thank you for being the chief storyline sounding board for me and I am sorry for making you turn off the volume to your favourite TV shows when I got the laptop out. 143 SBFH

All errors and omissions in this book are entirely mine and I take full responsibility for them. Sorry if that's the case but drop me a line via the contact form at
www.writingsfromasmallisland.weebly.com
and I will attempt to amend the errors.

Ian Yates
Crete - Oct '13

Mortui vivos docent - The dead teach the living.
- Anonymous

Life is like an autopsy... one piece at a time.
-Anonymous

CHAPTER 1

She knows if she stops moving she will die. That and fear is all the motivation she needs. The cuts on her arms, body and face are mixing with the sweat that is gushing from every pore. Her life fluids are draining away slowly and creating weakness when what she needs most now is strength. The torchlight flits back in her direction allowing her to see her breath steaming as it is pushed from her lungs. She runs on, not caring in which direction, knowing only that she has to stay away from the light. Her nakedness is not an issue anymore. She has been stripped of more than just her clothes over the previous ten days. Ten days of abuse and depravity that she did not think a human being could inflict upon another.

She is unable to get her bearings. The building she has been caged in is larger than she thought. Her bare feet slap against the bare concrete floor and she hears the echo of a huge room all around her. There is no natural light to see just how large is the area she has entered. She must have come through a door to get into this room but she did not see one. It must be some kind of warehouse or old factory building. Hands thrust out in front of her are the only reasons she does not run full speed into a wall.

Still moving, but more slowly, cautiously, she turns left and with her right hand she starts to follow the wall's path. It drops from smooth concrete to a ridged metal surface. A door!

Grasping desperately she finds a door handle. Expecting it not to yield she is astonished when it turns easily in her hands. Thinking of rusty hinges she slowly eases the door open. The opening reveals nothing but more blackness. With the door now fully open she pushes her hand through the gap only for it to crush painfully against a rough brick wall. It has been blocked.

She lets out an involuntary cry as she sees her chances drain away like her blood. It only attracts attention.

'She's in here!'

Torches streak through the darkness like laser beams in a science fiction movie.

The light finds her.

'There she is!'

She stops, frozen in the light like a rabbit. She drops her head, her shoulders slump and she starts to sob.

'Get the bitch. Use the cuffs and leg irons this time.' The voice she has learnt to fear.

She allows herself to be handcuffed and bound.

A different voice now. Younger sounding.

'She's gone, she's fucking out of it man. Look at her, she's broken. Forget the leg irons. It'll only slow us down. I'll get the cameras, you sort her out.' She knows this man as the one who is almost tender. He just uses her without the beatings. She is still sobbing silently as she is lead, surprisingly gently, back through the factory complex to the windowless room where the other women are.

The dead women.

CHAPTER 2

'How the hell do you manage to eat that stuff?'
I look up from my plate of snails, shallow fried with whole cloves of garlic. They have been fried in the finest olive oil I have ever tasted which is imported from a small town called Kolymbari in Crete, Greece. I know this because my brother Paul, who moved there last year after serving thirty years in the army, sends me the oil and I give it to the restaurant owner as part payment for his great food. That and I have a crush on his daughter and I am trying to keep him sweet. Julia and I have been dating for just over six months and things are looking good from my perspective. I'm not sure if the oil helps my case but as her father Nektarios is originally from a small town called Spilia just inland from Kolymbari, it can't hinder it.
My partner is looking at me with the disgust clear on his face. I pull one of the snails from its shell, spear a clove of the garlic alongside it, and hold it out for him.
'Try something new. You might like it.'
He pulls back as if I am holding a deadly snake out for him to kiss. I shrug and make a great show of my ecstasy as I chew on this small Greek delicacy.
'Pete, I'm sorry. There's been another one.'
He really knows how to spoil my appetite. Swallowing uncomfortably I push my plate away and wait for him to continue.

ONE PIECE AT A TIME

Jonathon Dawkins, or JD, has been my partner on the Homicide and Serious Crime Command (HSCC) for a little over two years. It is fair to say we work homicide well together even if we make a strange-looking couple. He is a squat, wedge-shaped figure from his love of pushing weights and I tower over his five and a half feet of pure muscle by almost a foot. And I don't push weights.

'She was found in the alley behind Valascos Bakery. Mutilated just like our last five victims and placed in three separate dumpsters.'

'The hands?'

JD looks down at his own hands flexing and cracking the knuckles.

'Yeah. Same as the rest. But this time we have a witness. A guy saw someone dumping the body.'

I stand and place a twenty on the table.

'Let's go.'

The uniforms are blocking the alleyway from curious onlookers and the less inquisitive press. Mobile phones and iPads are flashing away as the tourists revel in taking in another unexpected London show. The press know it will just be another 'No comment' moment until the details are released in the full statement. But they try and look interested anyway.

'DCI Peter Carter…any news if this is related to the body found last week?'

I look around and see Ann Clarke of The Metro looking over at myself and JD.

'Hi Ann, you pulling the late shift tonight?'

She smiles and I remember how her face looked after we made love. We used to have a thing together but she couldn't understand how I could keep secrets from her. Her job and mine were just not compatible.

'You know how it is Peter; I've got the boss on my back always after the next Ripper story. Exclusive this, exclusive that. He really grips my shit sometimes. Can you tell me, is this one of them?'

'You of all people know I can't discuss details of any ongoing investigations with the press Ann. As soon as we know any details of the incident here tonight we will issue a statement.'

'But as you are the lead investigator on the new Ripper I am assuming this is his latest victim.'

'You know what assumptions do to journalists careers Ann. Wait for the official statement.'

With that I follow JD into the alleyway and pull on a thin pair of surgical latex gloves that I always carry with me for occasions such as these.

The SOCO, or Scene Of Crime Officer, is standing to one side talking to the forensics lead investigator. In his white paper coveralls that look two sizes too big for him, Dr Graham Young is a strange looking character next to the uniformed officer. I attended a seminar on *Ballistics and the Effects on the Human Body* he presented in Leeds where he was based at the time. I made a point of seeking him out afterwards and I spent an interesting evening picking the brains of one of the world's foremost forensic scientists over a few pints of Guinness. I feel lucky to have him as part of our small team and it was not an accident that I persuaded him to consider a job with the London Metropolitan coroner's office when his contract expired 'up North'.

JD looks over to me, 'Peter, I'll check details with the SOCO. I know you and the Doc have a lot to catch up on.'

JD expertly eases away the SOCO and I make my way towards my old friend. We don't shake hands, even in our gloves, to try and stop any cross contamination.

'Doc, how is it looking here?'

'Good evening Peter, not a good one this. It looks at first sight to be another victim of our Ripper. I don't want to go on record until we do the full post mortem but indications are definitely running in that direction. We have the same level of dismemberment.'

I follow him as he walks into the alley and he continues his commentary like a local tour guide. All he needs to complete the picture is to hold a brightly coloured umbrella in the air above his head. All around us are plastic cards bearing the sequential numbers of the forensics teams investigation. The largest number I notice is 47. Forty seven clues or items of interest as to who has violated another human being in the most violent way.

Graham's commentary rolls on, 'The arms and legs are together in one location here, minus the hands that is.' He points to a green coloured dumpster which is being photographed by one of his men from the Evidence Recovery Unit.

'The head has been removed and placed in a small cotton drawstring bag, just as we saw before, in that area there, and the torso with hands inserted into the sexual organs is propped against the third bin here. She was found by a homeless man looking for scraps from the bakery. It didn't faze him much, he says he saw worse in Afghanistan. He reports he saw a man down here dumping stuff and he hoped it was food. He found more than he bargained for. He is down at the station waiting further questioning. JD took him down before coming to get you and he probably gave him a decent meal and a few hot cups of coffee too knowing JD. Female's age is anywhere from late teens to late twenties, bone structure and density will help with that, but that is my best guess for now. Decay of the body makes dating the time of death difficult, but anywhere over the last month is about all I can say for now. As with the other bodies I doubt we will be able to narrow it down. This guy likes to keep them around for a while after he has killed them.'

He looks me over, 'How are you doing after...'
I break in quickly, 'Doc I'm fine, just fine. Do we have a positive ID yet? Is it...?' I let the question hang.
'No. We are running a photo analysis, dental matching to follow and we are cross-checking with missing persons, but, her features have been distorted due to decay and also being badly beaten. There are also what looks like some small teeth marks in the fleshy parts of her face and we will try and get a match through dental records on the perpetrator but I do not hold much hope on getting a match. This is much worse than the others and shows an escalation in the violence against these poor girls. The worst part is I cannot say if the violence was carried out whilst she was still alive or, I hope for her sake, post mortem.'
We both stand and watch as two of the forensic team lift the brutalized torso, place it into a body bag and respectfully lay it down on a medical trolley. Two other trolleys with empty body bags stand nearby waiting for their own chilling cargo to be placed upon them.
'We have got to catch this bastard.' I whisper softly to myself. Graham, overhearing my out loud thoughts murmurs his agreement.
JD comes striding over after getting the latest news from the SOCO. His width appears to almost fill the small space of the alleyway as he gets closer.
'Not much else to report here Peter. Nobody at the bakery heard or saw anything and the security camera you see over the side door is a dummy one for deterrence only. Forensic are going to go over this place with the finest tooth comb they have in their inventory. The Doc here will be performing the autopsy tomorrow morning and the homeless guy who found the torso, an army veteran called Neal Stephens is at this moment having a snooze down at the station. I have him in an interview room as I know you will want to have a word with him sooner or later. Do you want to see him tonight?'

'This place is under control so why not. Doc, I'll catch up with you tomorrow. Thanks for the run through. I'll scratch a press statement together and await confirmation from you that this is another Ripper killing, of which it bears all the bloody hallmarks. You'll let me know if you find the same objects in the body.'

'Of course Peter, I will inform you straight away. I am almost hoping we do, otherwise we have two psychopaths running around out there.'

His words make the already cool night drop a few degrees more.

'OK JD, let's get back and see if we can get anything useful from your Mr. Stephens. I hope you got a receipt for his meal. You know Shirley in accounts will be all over you if haven't.'

He smiles, 'That's the plan Peter…that's the plan.'

CHAPTER 3

The Black Lion pub is fairly full. Young men and women with a day's work behind them letting off steam amid the old timers who sit stoically watching the muted TV set that is showing horse racing. The only movement they manage is raising their half of Guinness to their lips and checking form in The Racing Post.

Zoe Walker is standing near the unused pool table and laughing heartily at another unfunny joke her boss is telling her. Richard is assistant manager at the Staples where Zoe works as the secretary to both him and the branch manager. He has been trying to get into her knickers since she started the job six months ago and Zoe feels that tonight could be his lucky night. It all depends on Richard's answer to her asking for a pay rise. He said they should discuss it over a drink and she definitely knew where it was heading. As long as his wife didn't find out and cause trouble, as happened in her last post, it could be a mutually happy agreement but she can't afford to lose another job. A boss and his secretary may be the oldest cliché in the book, but if it pays the rent and she gets to have a few meals and drinks thrown in, where's the harm in that.

At 26 Zoe feels she should be allowed to have some fun and bugger the long term consequences. She does not want to settle down and have kids like most of her friends. She likes to party and she likes to stretch things to the limit.

She leans into him and places her hand on his arm. Her breasts push into his chest as she has to stand on tip toe for her mouth to reach his ear.

'So what do you say we talk about that pay rise now?'

He doesn't move away but rather pushes his body closer to hers.

'I think now would be a good time. Do you want to do it here or somewhere a little quieter, like your place.'
'Tell you what Richard, buy me another drink and bring it over to that booth there. I'll be waiting for you and we can discuss your proposal in a little more privacy. Then we'll talk about other things.'
She stares unashamedly into his eyes and sees the arousal there. Pulling slowly away from his body she lets her hand drop from his arm and brush his crotch almost as if by accident. Her eyes locked on to his show it wasn't. She takes a small step backwards and turns towards the booth.
'Yeah. OK. Drink coming right up.'
Richard turns away and heads for the bar with thoughts racing through his head. Jesus she's a spicy one this Zoe, he thinks to himself. I mean I knew she was up for it with all that flirting but this is it, a few drinks, give her 50p an hour pay rise and then take her back to her place for some fun.
It doesn't take him long to get served at the bar and he walks triumphantly back to the booth and Zoe with a pint for him and a gin and tonic for her.
'There you go Zoe, I made it a double.'
He sits opposite her and smiles as he feels her leg caress his under the table. The touch sends small jolts of erotic electricity straight to his groin. He has to adjust his sitting position to avoid uncomfortable embarrassment.
'So Richard, working for you the last six months has been fun but I really need to earn more money or I will have to move on. I have a job in mind that has offered me a position but I feel loyal to you, and I know you would like me to stay. What can you give me to make me even happier?'
The teasing of his leg does not stop.
'Tell me Richard, what have you got that will make me come in your office every day?'
The innuendo is so obvious even Zoe is surprised at her bluntness.

'Zoe, I…uh…I can give you a pay rise of 50p an hour starting tomorrow.'

Zoe's leg is pulled away sharply.

'Fifty fucking pence an hour. You have got to be kidding me right. Fifty fucking pence!'

'Zoe you have to understand that you have only been with us 6 months. Management will not allow any more than that. It's even in your contract.'

Zoe snorts with derision and takes a long drink from her G&T.

'Fuck management and fuck you. Or more accurately, fuck management and don't fuck you. I am going to have you up on harassment charges, how do you think your wife will react to that?'

'Zoe, don't be overdramatic there's no harassment. I played along with you, you led me along. You have…'

'Shut up Richard. If you can't offer me a better deal, even if it comes out of your own pocket, well I will have no choice but to ruin you. I'm going to the loo and by the time I come back you had better have something else for me. Trust me Richard, I'm worth it, and I'm not talking about my working skills here.'

Richard watches Zoe stride around the corner and off towards the toilets. I am in so much shit now, he thinks. One half of him wants her to stay no matter the cost, the other half wants to see the back of her. His problem is the harassment charge placed against him by one of his employees when he first started working for the company. Even though that incident occurred before he was married that would not matter to the bosses and HR and especially to his wife if she found out about it. Richard rapidly realizes that Zoe holds all the aces, he must do what she asks. He can explain to his wife a little of his wages being lost as cutbacks by the company due to the financial crisis.

'That decides it then.' He says out loud, 'I'm fucked.'

He takes a long pull on his pint and sits back to wait for Zoe to return. He is still there an hour later before he understands he has been stood up.

As he storms out of the pub his mind is in a whirl as he wonders what games Zoe is playing with him and what she has in store for him over the coming days, weeks even months. He hails a cab and worries all the way back home to his wife.

CHAPTER 4

'So JD, you and Shirley. I have to say I never saw that coming.'
I don't want to talk about the case and I definitely don't want to talk about my personal life, so I railroad the conversation. JD smiles at me with what he calls his film-star smile. All teeth and squinty eyes. He likes to think he has a close resemblance to Vin Diesel but in reality, even in the best light, he bears more than a passing likeness to Alfred Hitchcock. Albeit a buff Alfred Hitchcock.
'We got talking at Paddy O'Hara's retirement party and found we both have a passion for musicals.' He gives me a sideways look, 'Don't give me that grin, she likes going to the West End and so do I. So I took her out last week to see a show.'
I raise an eyebrow, 'Go on, what did you take her to see? Les Miserable, Cats, Miss Saigon…what?'
His hands flex on the steering wheel.
'Mama Mia.'
I can't help but burst out laughing and JD joins in with me.
'But you hate ABBA. I believe I have even heard you say it is, what was it now… aural torture.' I continue chuckling to myself, 'So how did the date go?'
'Apart from the music? Good. I get to pick the next show and I'm going to put her through the hits of Queen with We Will Rock You. Try and get my own back.'
'A second date, I didn't realise it was a serious relationship. I'd best dust off my morning suit and get a new hat.'
'It will be the fifth actually.' JD says quietly.

For JD this is something of a milestone. His relationships normally end pretty quickly as he seems to spend more time looking after his physique at the gym than in entertaining and looking after women. A fact that most women don't seem to care for. I can count on the fingers of one hand the number of relationships that he has had that have lasted more than three dates. Hell, I can count on the fingers of one finger the relationships that have lasted that long.

'Good for you mate. Shirley's a nice girl. Do you want me to set you up with a meal at Nektarios' place? My treat.'

JD shakes his head like he's listening to a child.

'Look Peter, I can sit through a performance of Mama Mia, but Greek food with all that lamb's heads, snails and garlic fried in olive oil. I like you Peter I really do, let's try and keep it that way. How about a nice Italian meal? Zafforellis or somewhere like that. I'll keep the receipt and bill it to you.'

Now it's my turn to shake my head, 'If I could afford Zafforellis I would be investigated for being on the take. We'll compromise on a nice bottle of Montelpuciano and a bargain bucket on a park bench of your choice.'

'Sounds like a deal to me just so long as I get to choose the park bench.'

I smile and try and forget the reason we are driving through London on a cold night like this.

'Peter…I haven't said it before but..'

'Then don't.' I snap back. 'Don't say it.'

'Peter, are you sure you can continue on this case?'

I know why he says this. This is why I tried desperately to steer the conversation from the beginning. People are seeing the pattern emerging in the murders. A woman, no, a girl goes missing. A month or two later she turns up having been abused, dismembered, decayed and rotten. I see people look at me and I can almost hear them think to themselves, 'How long has his sister been missing? How long until she turns up in some alleyway, chopped to pieces by some lunatic?'

I turn and look out of the window hoping with less certainty each day that it won't happen to Helen, my sister, missing now for three weeks.

'JD, until Helen turns up safe and well people are going to talk. It's not the first time she's disappeared for a while and this is no different to those other times. I can't believe she is mixed up in all this, I won't believe it. So I will continue this investigation and I will do all I can to catch this bastard before any more girls are hurt. End of conversation.'

The hands flex again on the steering wheel and we continue the rest of the journey in silence.

Neal Stephens is sitting behind the metal table in interview room number one, a cup of the cheap filter coffee from the machine outside in front of him. A flimsy and empty plastic plate and only slightly sturdier cutlery are pushed off to one side. At least he has been fed and watered, I think to myself. There are three of us in the observation room, myself, JD and the uniformed custody sergeant.

'Has anyone spoken to him yet?'

'Not yet sir,' the custody sergeant replies, 'apart from the few questions on the scene by Mr Dawkins here. He was brought here about two hours ago, no complaints. At least he's in the warmth and he has all the hot coffee he can handle. Nice chap actually sir, he...'

'OK sergeant. Thanks for keeping an eye on him. JD, let's go. I want you to talk to him as you've already got a rapport with the guy. I don't want us getting complacent with him as he's the only person so far who's witnessed anything.'

'No problem. Are we treating him as a suspect or as a potential witness?'

'Just a witness for now. Sergeant, can you run a full background check on this guy. Focus especially on his army records. I want to see if he has any history of violence, criminal violence I mean, during his time in service. See if you can get his conduct records as well. Cheers.'

The custody sergeant walks out of the observation room muttering under his breath. I don't care if I have just ruined his quiet evening, Neal Stephens is the best chance we have of catching our killer and I want to know as much about him as possible.
'Right then JD, it's your lead. Has he been searched?'
JD looks crestfallen, 'He was a witness, I didn't think…'
'Jesus JD! Shit. We know nothing about this guy and you don't even think to ask him to empty his pockets before bringing him here. What about forensics on his clothes, fingerprinting…anything.' I stare at him but he won't look at me.
'Get the fingerprinting kit, DNA swabs, evidence pack up and a change of clothes for him. We will have to assume he has been all over the crime scene.'
'Pete, Peter. I'm sorry. The first thing I did was physically check the body with the forensic techs to ensure,' JD pauses, 'to ensure it wasn't Helen. Then I brought him here and came and got you. I was just so relieved it wasn't her that…'
'And you have the nerve to ask me if I should be working on this case. For fucks sake JD get a grip on yourself. Let's do this.'
As JD rushes off to get the items required to eliminate Stephens from our enquiry or provide us with evidence of his guilt, I force myself to breathe slowly. It is oversights like this that cause overpaid and out of touch judges to let criminals go free.

CHAPTER 5

Zoe's throat is on fire. She is lying naked on a cold, hard floor but she does not realise her nakedness yet. She manages to get up on all fours and struggles to get air into her lungs. She wants to breathe deeply but the vomit rising to her mouth stops her doing so. She can do nothing but let it come and watches the contents of her stomach splatter on to the concrete floor as if through someone else's eyes.
'Let it come, breathe through your nose if you can. Short breaths and when it stops, whatever you do, don't scream. It will only hurt your throat more and we can't be heard in here.'
Looking over to the source of the voice, Zoe sees a young woman, also naked, curled up on the floor staring at her. Through her mind's fog she starts to become aware of her surroundings and her own naked vulnerability. Before she can answer or ask the stranger anything more, vomit is purged from her lips.
'Can you at least turn the other way when you are sick. There's not much clean space in here.'
Zoe does as the girl asks and turns her head away only for her to look straight into the clouded eyes of another face. The terrifying death mask of a woman who has only gaping wounds where her legs should be. She lets out a silent scream as she gags on more vomit and tries to move away. Her body is too weak for this rapid movement and she collapses into her own mess, coughing and crying in equal measures.
She hears an animalistic wail and vaguely comprehends it is coming from her own mouth. She flinches as a hand touches her on the shoulder. It is a gentle touch and she stops her keening as the other woman uses her hands to rub feeling back into her body.

'It's OK. It's going to be OK. You get used to it, you get used to them. You don't see them after a while.'

Zoe turns to face her comforter, 'See them? What do you mean, them?'

In the dim light the woman nods in the direction over Zoe's shoulder.

'Them. The three dead girls that are in here with us. There were more but now just three. Just three unless you upset the people that come to get us. Then there will be four.'

It is said flatly, no emotion in the voice at all. That is what scares Zoe more than if it was screamed out in terror.

'When I woke up, just like you now, there were two dead girls and four live ones. The ones who fight, who show spirit, they let live. The ones who give up...' she lets the sentence trail off. It does not need saying.

'How did I get here?' Zoe croaks through her raw throat, 'What happened?'

'I wish I knew hon. They use some sort of drug, that's why you are feeling what you feel now. I have heard them say it is ACE. Everyone comes round the same way, sore throat, banging head and sickness. It will pass.'

'How many have you seen? How long have you been here?'

There is a pause and the other girl starts sobbing gently.

'I don't know how long it has been. Three weeks, four weeks maybe.' She wipes her eyes with the back of her wrist and her voice turns cold and emotionless again. 'But there have been three other girls like you. You are the fourth since I was brought here.' She nods once more in the direction over Zoe's shoulder, ' Those are the other three.'

The two young women lay together on the cold floor both wondering when the door will open next. One is in terror because she knows what to expect when that happens, the other girls fear is because she does not.

CHAPTER 6

'Mr Stephens, this is DCI Carter who is leading the investigation into the disturbing scenes you found tonight. We would both like to thank you for your patience and ask that you can be as understanding as possible whilst we ask you some questions about the events you witnessed.'
Stephens clasps his hands, places them on the table and nods in my direction. He has not yet said a word since we entered the interview room. I allow JD to continue but notice that Stephens is watching me. He does not appear worried that for all intents and purposes, he is in police custody.
'Before we continue I must ask that we can get some samples from you. We need to take a sample of your DNA. That's very simple test, we just use one of these cotton buds to swab around the inside of your cheek, all very painless and quick. Then we must take your fingerprints so we can eliminate your prints from any of those that may be at the crime scene. We will also need to check your clothes and shoes, again to eliminate any forensic details that may arise at the scene. We would hate to see any mix up of evidence during this investigation as I am sure you are aware.'
He is still looking at me when he utters, 'Don't you want to search me and check for weapons, drugs and any other incriminating items. I have a knife. It is a 4 inch, non-serrated, folding Gerber.' He takes it out of his front-left jacket pocket and places it in front of him. 'It is used for protection and opening the occasional stubborn tin of food. The only drugs I have are a packet of ten Benson & Hedges. I have only smoked four.' these come from his top pocket along with a cheap disposable lighter, 'Any other items you find on me you are welcome to keep. But these,' he sweeps his hands to the objects on the table, 'these I want back.'

He winks and smiles at me and for the life of me I can't help but smile back. JD laughs out loud.
'OK Neal. They are yours to keep. Do you mind replacing your outer clothes with these ones? They are roughly your size I hope. We will leave the room and give you your privacy whilst you do so.'
Stephens jerks his thumb at the large mirror in the room, 'And let you watch through that window there anyway. Nah mate, you two can stay here and help me get these piles of crap off. I've been wearing them for weeks. Do you have any deodorant? I stink.'
As JD pops out to his locker to get a can of Lynx I help Stephens remove his clothes. He is wearing two jackets and it is only when the second comes off you can see just how skinny he really is.
'Apart from tonight Neal, when did you last eat a proper meal?'
He shrugs his shoulders, 'I dunno, maybe before I left the army.' He grins again.
The sweatshirt he has on bears the logo of the Royal Military Police. He sees me notice it and shrugs his shoulders.
'Do you want this off too?'
I nod my head, 'And then the jeans and no more. It's not a strip search.'
'No problem Mr Carter. No problem. Those ones there look better than mine anyway.'
He holds the jeans up to inspect them, holds them close to his face and takes a big sniff.
'Smell nice too. Any chance of a hot shower before I go back on the streets? After you have all the samples you need that is, I don't want to wash away any evidence.'
Again the contagious smile.
'I bet you were a good RMP weren't you Neal. Knew just how to keep on the good side of the squaddies. You have that feel about you. What were you, SI?'
As he tugs on the new pair of jeans he shakes his head.

'Me? Special Investigations? You're having a laugh. I was just a bloke in a uniform doing a job. Asked a few questions here and there, that was it.' He looks around. 'You haven't got a belt have you, these are a little big.'

'We'll get you one later. Why not sit back down and we'll talk about tonight.'

JD walks in with a can of Lynx Africa. The perfumed smell is overpowering in the small room as it is sprayed liberally but it is at least a little better than the overpowering body odour we had before.

'Great stuff, a true shower in a can. Now what can I tell you?'

JD looks to me, I nod and sit down opposite Stephens. JD glides his bulk into the seat next to mine and presses the record button to capture both audio and video from the interview room's two recording devices.

'Neal, can you tell us in your own words why you were in the alleyway behind Valascos bakery and how you came upon the body.'

Before Stephens can answer there is a knock on the door and it is opened by the custody sergeant. 'Sir, the information you asked for.'

In his hand he holds a small manila folder.

'That was quick. Thanks sergeant. Mr Stephens, please excuse me for one moment. My colleague will continue the interview without me. I shan't be too long.'

Rising from my chair I grab the evidence bags with Stephen's belongings.

'I'll have these back as soon as possible too.'

'Just the jackets, the rest you can bin. I'll keep these ones. Much nicer.'

I leave the interview room with the bags and take the manila folder from the sergeant.

Once outside and with the door closed I give the evidence bag to the now clearly pissed off sergeant.

'I suppose you would like me to take these downstairs and get them checked out for you would you sir?' His tone is heavy with sarcasm.

'That would be fantastic, I was only going to ask you to look after them while I go through his file, but as you clearly want to help out I have to say you're a true diamond.'

I give him my best smile but he just turns away, again muttering things I am supposed to hear but I just couldn't care less about.

'How come this came through so quick?' I ask waving the folder towards him.

He doesn't even turn around, 'It was already here. He was booked in last week after an altercation between him and another homeless guy. The other guy ended up in hospital with a broken wrist and forearm after apparently trying to steal his cigarettes. It was only because Stephens flagged down a uniformed patrol that we knew about it. Strange, he got himself into trouble by helping out the guy who was robbing him. Don't know who requested his file then but when I rang up the records office they said we already it and I found it in the custody inbox. You're welcome by the way.'

He waves over his shoulder as he turns the corner, I say waves because I won't acknowledge the middle finger salute he gave me.

I open the door to the observation room, take a seat and open the folder in front of me. This could take some time.

CHAPTER 7

Dr Graham Young is reading through his notes on the first five victim's autopsies in his Richmond apartment. The darker side of his occupation is clearly apparent in the décor and the ornaments that are scattered around the living room. There is a fine art print by Bob Orsillo labelled 'The Fortune Teller' in the entrance hall and various antique bottles with fading labels for 'cyanide', 'arsenic' and 'ether' on the shelves amongst others. He was once given a skull by a friend as a joke for a birthday, people soon caught on and he now has around eighty of them dotted around the place. There are real, human skulls, animal skulls, novelty wine goblets, he loves them all. He reasons that by looking at the real thing all day, coming home and seeing how art imitates life or, in this case, death helps him to relax. Divorced three times, he hates to say 'married three times' as it sounds too depressing, he now has what he considers the perfect bachelor pad. His apartment is just a short walk to the hallowed rugby ground of Twickenham and an even shorter walk to his favourite pub 'The Eel Pie' with great ales and even greater food. Pouring himself a second large glass of Skull Head Crystal Vodka over ice he opens the first file. Not to reacquaint himself with the details, they are far too harrowing for him to forget, but to see if there is something he has missed.

UNIDENTIFIED FEMALE
Date of Examination – 13-01-2013
Age – Approximation 20 – 25 years of age
He skims through the rest of the file until he comes to the main report.

PRIMARY VISUAL EXAMINATION (PVE)

Cause of death cannot be ascertained from PVE due to major trauma at the proximal areas of limbs of the victim's body post mortem. Body has been dismembered into 8 (eight) separate pieces. Head, legs and arms have been removed from the torso. The forearms show injuries to the proximal area and the distal location where the hands have been removed by a sharp, heavy instrument at the carpus. The hands have been inserted into the genitalia with some tearing of this locality apparent, unable to determine in PVE if this is pre or post mortem.

1. TORSO - shows signs of 3 (three) types of injury;
    i. Bruising – Extensive blunt instrument trauma.
    ii. Abrasion – Systematic to being dragged along a rough surface.
    iii. Incisions – Small incisions from a bladed instrument. Some have healed showing injuries occurred prior to death.

2. ARMS - show signs of defensive injuries with the same 3 (three) types of injury as the torso, as to be expected.

3. LEGS – As arms and torso.

4. SKULL - No visible signs of visible trauma to the flesh of the face or head.

5. HANDS – Uniform, circular bruising around the proximal extremities of the phalanges and multiple small incisions with scarring to the distal and ungual phalanges. Bruising appears to be caused by some kind of ring applied forcefully to the soft flesh.

All removed body parts show signs of being hacked or chopped away from torso with a heavy, sharp-bladed tool. First impressions would be some kind of axe or cleaver have been used, possibly both.

Graham closes his eyes and thinks back to his first feelings as he saw the body. What was missed? What did he see then with fresh eyes that now have now been dulled by the processing of four more, similar bodies. All show similar injuries, around the fingers, what on earth cause injuries like that? He thinks to himself. He looks down at his hands. The bruises on the fingers are consistent with a very tight ring cutting into soft tissue. Getting up he walks slowly over to a small three drawer cabinet on which a few of the more 'attractive' skull objects are displayed. Opening the middle drawer he takes out a small jewellery box and returns back to his chair. Inside are three wedding rings. All are slightly different sizes and he places one on each finger of his left hand ensuring a tight fit is present on each. As he flexes his fingers against the cold metal he feels the blood vessels begin to expand and tighten the ring even more firmly. As this happens he notices it is harder to flex his finger joints until it comes to a point where his hand looks like a claw. Realising it is becoming dangerously close to the point where he will need to cut off the rings or cut off his fingers, he takes the rings off. The blood pressure pounding back through his hand makes his fingers throb. He tries to imagine what purpose the rings could have.

Graham lets his mind wander. Bruises. Cuts. Pain. Looking down at the rings and his hand as it starts to regain its normal shape he thinks, claw. He hurriedly grabs all the photographs of the torsos and looks at the tiny incisions inflicted upon them. Comparing these incisions with those on the fingers shows the same size and shape. He slumps back in his seat, eyes again closed as he turns his face up to the ceiling. What if they are not defensive wounds on the fingers. What if they are caused by the rings. Could the ring be the weapon and as the fist is closed it cuts the tips and joints of the fingers. Unconsciously he is opening and closing his fingers as he peruses this line of thought. But why give these girls a chance to fight back, he asks himself. What would be the point?

ONE PIECE AT A TIME

Opening his eyes he reaches over to his glass and lets his eyes wander around the room as he tries to recall details. He finds himself staring at a cheap plastic skull with a dormouse emerging from an empty eye socket as he takes a large pull on the vodka. Another gift from a well-meaning colleague but he can't remember who. He can't put a face to the gift.

It hits him. The face! Why is the face untouched when the rest of the body shows so many signs of damage? Why does the killer not want the face damaged? He turns the pages of the documents before him and looks at more of the pictures taken during the autopsy. The whole body has been battered, cut and traumatised but the face is untouched. Each time he looks at another infliction of pain on the body, arms and legs he keeps coming back to the face. He checks all of the reports and photographs once again. There is just one of the deceased that shows signs of trauma to the head. This is the only one that shows bruising and on his further inspection it was revealed to be caused by a hairline fracture of the cheek bone prior to death. He thinks back to the new victim earlier in the evening and the beating to the face and bite marks to the cheekbone. Is this an escalation in violence or something more? Perhaps this is the first cry for help that the psychologists say every serial killer will unconsciously produce at some time sooner or later. Are the bite marks a way for the killer to say 'Come catch me, here I am.'

Graham shakes his head and takes another sip of his vodka and talks to no-one but himself,

'Leave the mind games to the professionals. You get the answers from the dead, stop second guessing the living.'

He forces himself to read the most surprising find of the autopsy report. The most chilling find of the whole investigation as far as he is concerned.

Tissue and DNA matching of hands to rest of body tissue is inconclusive. The hands that have been inserted into the genitalia do not belong to the deceased.

I repeat, the hands DO NOT match the tissue or DNA found in the rest of the body.

He had underlined this last sentence to ensure it caught the investigating officers attention. This was the first autopsy but it was discovered that all women were found with someone else's hands instead of their own. What chills Graham is that while they have matched three of the five pairs of hands to the other victims found, two sets of hands belong to people they have not yet managed to identify. Two unfound victims of the new Ripper.

He finishes the rest of his vodka and closes the folders as if to block the remaining details from his mind. Graham knows another drink will not help him sleep any easier but he pours himself an extra large measure anyway. The tumbled thoughts and theories of his overactive mind keep him awake until just before dawn.

CHAPTER 8

Neal Stephens was a corporal in the Royal Military Police before being discharged after 8 years. Joining in July 1997 he had served in the Falklands, Oman and, just before he left the services voluntarily, Iraq. There were no indications that he had any disciplinary record whilst serving in the military and he had kept a clean sheet as a 'civvy' up to the altercation last week. What was strange, I thought, was that whilst his time in the UK, the Falkland Islands and Oman were extremely well documented, including a citation from the Commander British Forces South Atlantic, only dates were included for his Iraq tours. June 2003 – September 2003 and then February 2004 – February 2005. That was it, a blank time period of twenty months from when he first arrived to when he left the country for the second time in 2005. He left the army 3 months after returning home, in May 2005. Alarm bells started to ring in my head.
What was it he said, 'I asked a few questions here and there.' I think back to the cases of alleged abuse to prisoners in the coalition forces detention centres. Could he have been involved somewhere along the line and the military were keeping it quiet? Was he pushed out after being caught doing something that was against the Geneva convention, but due to other high profile incidents, the army covered it up. I look up as I catch JD asking Stephens to repeat something.
'Can you once more describe the events leading up to how you came across the person you saw in the alleyway and then we will discuss his actions when he saw you.'
Stephens is still looking calm and collected, his hands folded on the table in front of him. His eyes drift off slightly to the right as he remembers the events that brought him to the interview room.

'I was looking for some food, I guess that much is obvious. The bakery is normally a pretty good bet if you get there early enough but I was late this evening, sidetracked by a bloke who wanted a talk. You know, at first he was one of those good Samaritan types. If you let these guys talk and give them a nod at the right times you normally come away with a fiver at least. Anyway this guy just kept talking and talking and what it comes down to is he wants to take me home for the night. Wants to humiliate his wife with a total stranger. Now I know some guys are into that but not me. I told him to piss off when he started offering money, but he kept on saying how much she deserved to be used and abused by someone like me. I walked away when he offered me £100 to be rough with her. I mean that's not right is it. No man should treat his wife like that. But he won't give up, says she likes to fight back and he needs someone who has been around the block a bit. *'You look like the sort of bloke who could do that.'* he says. Now that pisses me off. I start yelling at him and push him away. At least this time he takes the hint but not before telling me I've just missed the chance of a lifetime. Sick bastard.'

'Have you seen this man before and did he see what happened in the alleyway?' JD prompts.

'I'd recognise him again if I saw him but I don't think he saw anything 'cos he went off in the opposite direction. Heading towards the East End. Probably looking for another sicko to drag into his fantasies. He probably found one up there with no problems.'

JD nods and takes down a few things in a small notebook, 'So what happened when you parted company, where did you go then?

'Well the bakery was just around the corner but I had already seen a few of the guys head away from the alleyway. I figured there wasn't going too much left, but you never know right, they could have missed something. As I walk in I see a big guy with a bag in his hand. One of those cotton ones you put bread in, and I think my luck is in. It looked like a full loaf the size of it in his hands. Anyway he throws this bag in the dumpster and turns to walk away, he doesn't go to the bakery door, but heads down the alleyway to me. Knowing now what it was, Jesus, he doesn't even look worried. He fucking smiles at me and says *Have a nice evening.* I mean 'Have a nice fucking evening', how cool was that guy. Seeing me didn't faze him at all.'

Although he tries to hide it in his body language, I can hear the eagerness in JD's voice, 'And you got a good look at the guy?'

'He was as close to me as you are now. He's a weights warrior like you. A little broader in the shoulders but he is taller so I guess he has the advantage over you. I would say he is 5'11" give or take an inch and has a Scottish accent. One of those soft ones, maybe Aberdeen region.'

I raise an eyebrow, nothing in his file says he has been anywhere near Aberdeen. Luckily JD also picks up on this. 'Why do you say Aberdeen? That's a bit specific for a one sentence greeting.'

Stephens seems suddenly interested in the table top.

'I had a few guys I worked with in the army who came from the area. My best mate was from a little place called Elgin, just North of the Granite City. This guy had the exact same accent. You don't forget things like that. When we did his funeral just the sound of his brother's voice when he talked had me in tears every time.' He looks JD in the eye, 'Is that specific enough for you?'

JD nods, it's his turn to become infatuated with the table. 'Continue with what happened next please.'

Stephens leans back in the hard-edged chair.

'He left and I walked on to see what goodies he had left. Figured he had just closed up the store and was going home. How wrong was that assumption?' He asks himself.
He takes a sip of now cold coffee.
'I don't make it to the bin as I see the body,' he pauses, 'I see the torso of that poor girl. I've seen things like that before but only after suicide bombs or IEDs. This was cleaner, almost sterile. I turn around to shout out for help and see the guy at the end of the alleyway. He's grinning at me. The bastard is grinning at me, then he just turns away like he hasn't got a care in the world and walks off to the right, off in the direction of the tube.'
JD turns to look straight at the observation mirror, he has a complex victorious smile yet almost a lost look on his face.
'Would you be able to use a computer aided photofit to identify this person?'
He turns back to Stephens who has also turned to stare at the mirror.
'Definitely.' It's all the reply I needed to hear as I realise I have the same look on my face as JD had a few seconds ago.
'OK Neal, before we start that I need the names of the people you saw leave the alley. We need to check their stories too and find out if they witnessed anything.'
Stephens snorts and looks at JD with incredulity, 'Names? Jesus man, nobody has a name out there. We are just faceless bundles of clothes that disappear during the day and try to get through another night. I only know they are like me because of the way they walked and the clothes they wear. Sorry boss. I can't give you any names or even tell you where they doss down. Sorry.'
I watch in contemplative silence as JD leads our only witness out of the interview room with a glimmer of hope in my heart that we may be on the verge of breaking this grisly case wide open. I know from experience to expect it to be false hope, but the glimmer is there none the less.

CHAPTER 9

I am once more sitting in my office going through the missing persons files. Going through Helen's file to be more precise. Helen was last seen leaving her apartment by her flatmate, Ewelina, who says she saw her getting in a black cab exactly three weeks ago today. I check my watch and correct myself, three weeks yesterday. Ewelina has no idea where she was going or who she was going to meet. Apparently Helen was cagey with her about the whole thing and just told her it was an opportunity too good to miss and she would be back in a few hours. Nothing has been seen or heard from her since. It was Ewelina that reported Helen missing two days later.
We are not a close family, our parents divorced when we were all quite young. Paul was the oldest at fifteen, I was twelve and Helen was five. By some strange reasoning of the court we were divided up like pieces of property during the divorce with Helen going to live with our father whilst Paul and I stayed with our mother. We would swap around for one weekend a month which we all dreaded. The questioning about our father by our mother was too much for us at that age. Helen would get a whole weekend of interrogation about his life whereas I would get a week of it when I returned home. I coped with it by throwing myself into my studies, Paul left home and joined the army at 16, Helen didn't manage so well.
At 15 years old she ran away from our father's house and went missing. I had just passed out of the police training college the year before and was still trying to find my feet on the streets of London with the Metropolitan Police. What I found instead was my sister selling herself on the streets for drug money.

Our mother was distraught, not at the fact that Helen had gone missing, but because she had sullied the family name. She blamed our father for not controlling his daughter. I still remember that phrase, '*His* daughter.' It was just like her to blame him for both their parenting failures. To his credit he persuaded Helen to go into rehab and get help. She came out a different person, she was stronger, more self assured. I am still not sure whether it was her time on the streets and not the six months in therapy that changed her from a lost girl into a strong, young woman.

Now, twelve years later, she is running her own personal fitness training business with a sideline of self defence courses for women. I can't see her running back to the streets when on the surface everything seems to be going so well for her. I wish I knew the details of what was going on in Helen's life, but I have been too occupied with the job that family members and friends have all taken a back seat. JD and Graham are the only true friends I feel I have and they are colleagues in the same position as I am. Maybe that is why we are so close. We all see and experience the same things that we can relate to how each other feels outside of work.

The cab driver that picked Helen up outside her apartment states he remembers dropping her off at Kings Cross station, a notorious area for local prostitutes, but I must not think back to her dark days. The GPS tracker in his cab backs up his statement and the timings all relate to Ewelina's version of events. CCTV shows her walking away from the station and then we lose her.

I put her file down and look at the others piled on my desk. Even in the days of computers, databases, cloud technology and the ever present internet search, we still rely on hard copies of everything. It still amazes me that each year over 300,000 people are reported missing in the UK, that is over 850 per day. The statistics are staggering. The Metropolitan Police alone have over 42,000 missing person reports each year and over 40% of those are young women between the ages of 15 to 40. That is what I am up against. That is what Helen is up against. I realise that statistically speaking there is very little chance of her being a Ripper victim, but the chance and the gnawing in my stomach remains.

I have concentrated on the reported missing cases in our area from the last seven weeks, four weeks before we found our first victim. This time period relates to the approximate time period our killer seems to be keeping the victims before dumping their bodies. In this seven week time frame there were over 7,500 missing person reports. Removing all missing males reduces this number to 3,900 and narrowing down the age groups to those women between 17 and 30 years of age brings it down to 845. That is seventeen young women reported missing each day over the last seven weeks.

Those found safe, in hospital or victims of fatal accidents or suicides reduces the challenge even more and as our killer has only chosen white females of a slim or athletic body type, I have the final reports on my table. Eighty three files where a young woman has been reported missing by a concerned family member or work colleague and all a potential victim of violence and dismemberment. My sister's file is the first one I read each time but my team are more impartial. There are three police officers working meticulously through each file, chasing leads and speaking to parents, husbands, colleagues and friends to glean any information that may be crucial to our case. Even I have been interviewed to review the details of my sister's disappearance. I was not much help.

Of our five victims we have identified just two. Both were prostitutes that had been booked by the police over the past year. Victim number one is a 19 year old girl who was known to us by her street name, Indya, real name Alison McCormick. She was identified by fingerprints found from the hands which were with the body of victim number three. Indya was never reported missing, so much for statistics I think. No family or friends to release the body to, so she is still in the morgue with the hope that we will find someone before we have to release her body to the city's undertakers. The hands that were with Indya's body have been matched to our fourth victim with no identification as yet.

The fingerprints that identify 28-year-old Valerie Ross as one of our victims were found with body number one. She is still classified as missing as we have not yet matched her tissue or DNA to any of the bodies that have been found so far. We are hoping she is still alive but have resigned ourselves to the alternative. We had more luck with tracing her family as when she was booked she gave a home address in Blythe near Newcastle. Her father, Grant Ross, a larger than life IT consultant reported her missing last year to his local police station. When she was booked in for soliciting he received a call from the local constabulary informing him his daughter was alive and well and living in London. I can only imagine his relief and his despair at hearing the details of her arrest. Valerie dropped back off the grid until her hands turned up three weeks ago. Her father turned up in London last Tuesday demanding action and answers. I had no answers to give him except the conviction that we are doing all we can to apprehend the people who had committed this atrocity against his daughter. We sat in my office and I listened to him sob his heart out as he described his daughter to me and provided us with photographs of her that weren't police mug-shots. We got through half a bottle of Laphroaig that I keep in my desk drawer for just such occasions. As he left he shook each and every team members hand and thanked them for working so hard to find his daughter. On the way back to his hotel he jumped in front of the number 31 bus near Primrose Hill. He died at the scene, another victim of the Ripper.
Our other three women have yet to be identified and I hope we get some results from the autopsy tomorrow. We have matched most of the hands' tissue with the victims and I look at the table in front of me for confirmation. I only hope that our new victim pairs up the remaining blanks in the table. If not we will be awaiting more bodies and I do not want to think what that means for the other missing girls.

Victim No.	1	2	3	4	5	6
Date Body Found	13/01/13	18/01/13	20/01/13	N/A	01/02/13	07/02/13
Positive ID	Alison McCormick (Indya)	TBC	TBC	Valerie Ross	TBC	TBC
Hands/Body Match	No Body Found ID Vic 4	To Body 6	To Body 1	N/A	To Body 2	To Body 5
Hands Found	From Body 3 20/01/13	From Body 5 01/02/13	TBC	From Body 1 13/01/13	From Body 6 07/02/13	From Body 2 18/01/13

I rub my eyes and watch the digital clock on my wall change from 04:24 to 04:25. I take the cot bed, light duvet and pillow out of the bottom drawer of my filing cabinet and set it up on the floor of my office. Ensuring my alarm is set for 06:45 I get my head down for the night. Even with the images running rampant through my brain, I fall asleep the instant I lay my head on the pillow. My sleep, unsurprisingly, is a disturbed one.

CHAPTER 10

The door is thrown open and light floods the small room, blinding the two women. Zoe hears something clatter across the floor towards her.
'You know what to do. Bang on the door when it's done.'
She vaguely recognises the accent. The man who followed her into the toilet at the pub. She never saw his face, just heard him say something about her being 'up for it'. As she turned around she now remembers a heavy cloth going over her face, then she woke up here.
'What does he want us to do?' she asks her fellow hostage.
A sigh and a small sob escapes from the other girls lips and a metallic scraping sound is made as she picks up what was thrown into the room.
'Grab a body and bring it over here. This isn't going to be easy, but just think of it as meat. We are just cutting up a piece of meat.'
Zoe cannot believe what she is hearing.
'You can't be serious. They want us to...they want us...they..' Zoe breaks down into tears.
'Stop crying. If you piss him off he will come in here and make us both sorry. Bring that one here. Hold the arms out for me.'
The strength in the voice gives Zoe hope. Still crying she crawls over to the nearest body. The body with no legs. She grabs it, she can't think of the body as a 'her', under the armpits and drags it back into the middle of the room.
'I don't know you but I'm sorry.' Zoe whispers.

'Her name is Bernadette. She is from Bournemouth and she ran away from home six weeks ago and ended up in here. She died last week. I promised to remember her name, I promised to remember all their names just like I will remember yours Zoe. The girl in the corner is Anne-Marie, the girl beside her with no hands is Valerie.'

Zoe looks up at her companion, 'What's your name so I can remember it.'

The laugh is mocking and chills Zoe to the core.

'You won't need to remember my name. Only one of us is getting out of this alive, but as you ask. My name is Helen. Helen Carter.'

The sound of a cleaver cutting through flesh and bone reverberates around the small, dark room. Bernadette's body rocks with the blows inflicted upon it as Helen rains down the heavy blade to remove the limbs. Helen's laughter is the sound of insanity let loose, it almost blocks out the sound of Zoe's screams.

CHAPTER 11

'What the hell do you think you are doing Peter?'
The indignant tone of my immediate superior, Superintendent Patricia Wilks, breaks me from my disturbed slumber on the floor of my office. I raise my head slightly and open one eye.
'Morning boss. How are you today?'
I check my watch, 06:44. Great, just fucking great, I think to myself.
'Peter, again. Just what the hell do you think you are doing? You look like crap and this office stinks. My God Peter, the Commissioner is coming here this morning to get the up-to-date information from you before the press conference on the Ripper case, and you…you're a mess. He's going to want to meet with you to see what leads we have and he's not going to be impressed when he sees you dossing down in here.'
The alarm on my phone starts to play my wake-up call. I clamber for it to try and stop it before it goes on too long. I don't manage it and the superintendent is serenaded by the words and music of 'Fuck da police' by NWA.
She walks from my office shaking her head, 'He is coming at 7am, you have 15 minutes to get your shit sorted out. I'd best hurry if I were you.'
She almost walks straight into JD who is carrying two cups of coffee, a polystyrene box and an A4 folder.
'Morning boss, how's things?'
Her gaze makes him hurry past without another word.
'Who rattled her cage?'
He sees me propped up on one arm in my cot bed and bursts out laughing, 'Busted. Here's breakfast for you. Scrambled egg on rye. I thought you should try a bit of protein for a change. Man, you look like shit.'

He plonks his considerable bulk down in one of my chairs and watches me tidy up my temporary bedding arrangements whilst sipping his coffee. Turning back to him I watch as he points down to the folder on my desk.
'Thought you might like to see this. Stephens came through a treat on the photofit. I have had the night-shift guys trying to cross match an ID, nothing yet but it's early days.'
I sit down across the desk from him, 'Have you managed any kip?'
JD shrugs his shoulders. It looks like they are trying to break free from his jacket.
'An hour or two, maybe less.' He sees me looking at him, 'What? Are you the only one who is allowed to burn the candle at both ends. Even the Doc came in early. He's doing the autopsy on the latest girl now. Said he couldn't sleep so he might as well do something constructive. The poor bastard looks worse than you, almost.'
I grab the coffee cup and pull the folder towards me. Before I can open it my desk phone rings. Caller ID shows it to be Dr Young.
'Morning Doc, how's the autopsy going?'
'How do you know that I have...Oh, I see, JD is with you. Thank him for the breakfast for me please. The eggs are delicious. I have some news for you Peter, I wanted to let you know first, that is, before the report was handed in. We have a preliminary identification on the bite marks we found on the victim last night. There is a 95% match, which as you know is far above what is required in a court of law. I'm sorry to say this Peter, but the bite marks match the dental records for your sister Helen. She was with this girl when she died.'
Graham continues speaking to me but I don't hear any more of what is being said. I hand the phone numbly over to JD and put my head in my hands. The nightmare has just taken a new, unwelcome twist.

I don't notice JD making notes or hanging up the phone. His hand on my shoulder jerks me out of my almost catatonic state.

'We have another match on the hands and we have identified this victim. And they found the same object inside the body.' Each victim so far has had a small, plastic ball, like a bingo callers ball, inserted into the vagina. Each one has been numbered, the first was 10. They have been counting backwards with each body we have found.

'The ball was numbered 5, Peter. We have four more victims to find before who knows what comes next and now we know Helen is one of them.'

'Are the hands Helen's?' It is as if someone else is asking the question.

A shake of the head.

'They belong to our victim number three. The girl we found on 20th January. The body from last night is a woman who went missing four weeks ago, a Claire Shannon. She dropped her daughter off at school and has not been seen since. The doc managed a dental match from her and we are getting the ex-husband in for a positive ID later this morning. I don't envy the poor guy seeing his wife like that.'

'Good morning gentlemen. Tell me we have something positive to tell the media scrum that is developing over this case. What can you tell me about the latest victim and I hear we have a witness. I need to know everything.'

The Commissioner sits himself down at my desk, grabs JD's coffee and starts to tuck into my breakfast.

'I'm ravenous, had a late night with Boris and the South Korean ambassador last night at their embassy. All dodgy food and weak wine.' He looks up, a plastic fork full of scrambled egg half way to his mouth. He gestures with it, 'Continue gentlemen, continue.'

I take a second to compose myself, look at JD with eyebrows raised and then share what we have so far with the head of the Metropolitan police service who has just stolen my breakfast. Standing behind him Superintendent Wilks is taking notes furiously.

Ninety minutes later we are all sitting down behind a long table in front of the national and international media. There is nothing like a serial killer to really get the floodlights and flashlights of the associated press going.
'Ladies and gentlemen, we will shortly begin the press conference. I ask that you wait for the statement to be completed by Metropolitan Police Commissioner Derek Temple before asking any questions.' Superintendent Wilks is in her element in front of the press. 'Also with us today is Detective Chief Inspector Peter Carter and Detective Inspector John Dawkins who are the officers in charge of the investigation, and myself, Superintendent Patricia Wilks of the Serious Crimes and Homicide Unit. You should all have a press pack that has been prepared for you by my office and we will give you a moment to review this before the conference begins.'
As Wilks sits down the Commissioner leans over to her, 'Could you get me some water please Patricia. They have forgotten to place it on the table again. Thank you.'
I try not to smile as my boss rises and is forced to perform this menial task. The Commissioner catches me in the act.
'So Peter, Patricia causing you headaches is she? Good. She can be a right pain in the arse at times I know, but she is good at her job. Don't forget that, also don't forget that she is the youngest Super ever in the Met. Remember Peter, she is your boss and loyalty is a trait that is reciprocated in this job. Something worth its weight in gold when the press and, even worse, the mayor start baying for blood because the investigation is going too slow for them.'

'Yes sir.' It's all I can think of to say. The warning is apparent. If there are not any answers soon then it will be my head on the chopping block whilst the superiors moan about budget cuts and under-manning. We wait five more minutes and then Commissioner Temple stands. The general chatter around the room stops immediately.
'Good morning ladies and gentlemen. I can confirm reports that last night we found a body in the Metropolitan jurisdiction that bears similarities to five other bodies we have found over the last four weeks. We are appealing for anyone who has any information about these horrific crimes to come forward and help the police with their enquiries.' He holds up two photographs, 'We are also appealing for anyone who has been in contact with these two women, Alison McCormick, also known as Indya to her friends, and Valerie Ross. If anyone has been in contact with these women over the past six months they should contact the Crime Hotline, the number is behind me and should be playing across the bottom of your TV screens.'
He pauses and places a hand on my shoulder.
'I shall now pass you over to DCI Carter, the head of this investigation.'
I remain sitting. On the screen behind me a photofit image of the man identified by Neal Stephens appears.
'We are looking for this man who was seen in the area last night, near where the latest victim was found. We warn the public to be on their guard as this man is considered highly dangerous. If you see this man you should contact the police immediately. Do not try to apprehend, follow or confront him, but please call 999 and relay his whereabouts. If you recognise this man, please call the Crime Hotline number. It is totally anonymous if you wish it to be. We believe this man to be the killer of six women from the London area and he is our prime suspect. I promise that all leads will be investigated and there is a reward of £20,000 that is available to the person that provides information which results in his arrest.'

I pause, now comes the hard part. A different image appears behind me. A young woman smiling directly at the camera, a cloudless sky behind her.

'We are also appealing for any information and sightings on this woman, Helen Carter. She disappeared from her home and was last seen in the Kings Cross area of London three weeks ago. We have reason to believe she has been in contact with at least one of our victims before they were murdered. We need to find her. We need to eliminate her from our enquiries and we also need to know that she is not another victim of this callous individual.'

I hear my voice beginning to crack, luckily for me so does JD. He stands up next to me.

'Ladies and gentlemen, DI Dawkins. This case is now the highest priority for all police forces throughout the United Kingdom. We have unparalleled levels of communication and cooperation across all districts and regions as never seen before.'

The screen changes again. On the left hand side of the screen is the photofit of our suspect and on the right are the three pictures of our two victims, Alison and Valerie and my sister, Helen. JD stares straight into the lens of one of the TV cameras.

'We will find this man. He will be arrested and he will go to jail for a long time. I promise you this.'

Superintendent Wilks stands up quickly.

'Thank you DI Dawkins. We will now accept a few minutes of questions, please raise your hand to keep it to just one at a time and please say who you are directing the question to.'

All hands shoot in the air at the same time. I watch as the Superintendent surveys the room before pointing at a target.

'Gina Morgan, Reuters, tell me Commissioner is there any news on the identification of the latest victim?'

'Yes, the body of the woman has been identified from the missing persons list. We have yet to inform all family members of the news and will not release details until they confirm their wishes over this tragic matter. Our condolences are with them at this terrible time.'
Another point of Wilks' finger.
'James Soper, Sky News. DCI Carter, I notice the same name and some similarities between the missing woman, Helen Carter and yourself. Is she related?'
The obvious pointed question catches me off guard. He knows we are related and wants a sound bite, wants his camera to catch the grief of a relative. I clear my throat before speaking, the room is silent.
'Yes. Miss Carter is my sister.'
The room erupts as questions fly out from all directions. Nothing Wilks can do will stop this scrum. She turns to me and mouths 'Get out.' Not in a bad way, but with compassion in her eyes.
I leave the frenzy behind me and JD follows me out to the relative calm of the corridor.
'That bastard knew.' He says.
I nod my head in dumb agreement and set off at a furious pace back to my office with JD in tow.

CHAPTER 12

'Have you seen Zoe today?'
The head poking around the door frame belongs to Martin Garret, the general manager of the Staples branch where Richard and Zoe both work.
'Um. No, come to think of it. But I've been busy with the stock-check preparations for this weekend. I thought she was working with you this morning.'
Richard did not want to say he hoped she was avoiding him and deliberately staying away from his office. He also did not want to reveal he was relieved when she did not show up for work this morning.
'Give her a ring at home will you Richard. Just make sure she's OK. With all this stuff going on with girls going missing and being murdered, it just worries me. It really gives me the creeps to think that somebody could do that to a human being. Did you see the news this morning?'
Richard shakes his head.
'A big press conference over the Ripper murders and it turns out the policeman in charge of the whole thing, well, it only turns out his sister is one of the missing girls. Terrible, just terrible.' Martin shakes his head. 'I hope Zoe is alright, probably just woman troubles again, but I have to admit I feel worried with what is going on. Let me know how she is when you ring her Richard, please.'
The head disappears from the door frame as Martin returns across the narrow hallway to his own office. Richard sighs and picks up the phone. He can't help but think how much easier his life would be if Zoe has been kidnapped by the Ripper. At least he would not have to confront his wife over the drop in pay he must take to keep Zoe happy.

After five rings the answer phone cuts in, 'Hi this is Zoe, sorry I'm not here right now, I'm either out having a great time or recovering from a great time and don't feel up to answering your call. Either way leave a message and I'll get back to you when reality kicks in. Thanks…..Beep.'

Richard leaves a short message asking Zoe to ring work when she can and hangs up. He picks his mobile phone off the desk and starts typing out a text message before he realises it was text messaging that got him into trouble the last time. He quickly deletes it along with her mobile number, places the phone in his pocket and makes his way to Martin's office.

'Uh Martin, no answer at Zoe's but I left a message on her machine. She could be ill or at the Drs I suppose. If I don't get a reply by lunchtime I will get one of her friends to pop round her flat and check up on her.'

'OK good. Now bring me up to date with the latest on the Brother printer order and what they are doing about the DOR's we have been receiving.'

Richard closes the door behind him and sits down with his boss. They both forget about Zoe as they discuss what must be done with a batch of 'Dead On Receipt' faulty printers that have been returned by customers.

CHAPTER 13

I am with JD watching the news coverage of the press conference that seems to be on a fifteen minute loop with Sky News. Each time I see the look on my face and my hasty exit from the room it looks to me like the retreat of a desperate man running away from a truth he can't handle. I am starting to believe that this is the case after the video's sixth run through. My phone rings, an internal call. I answer after the fourth ring. I think I know what's coming.
'Peter, Superintendent Wilks. Can you and DI Dawkins be at my office in fifteen minutes, there are things we need to discuss.'
She hangs up.
'Wilks' office, fifteen minutes, the two of us.'
JD nods his head slowly, 'Do you think…?' he lets the question trail off into the air.
'I don't know what else I should think JD. They're going to say I have too much of a personal interest in the case. They're going to pull me off it.'
JD looks at his watch. I notice it is a new one and smile. JD buys watches like most people buy cereals. The one he is wearing today is a nice titanium Tissot T-Touch with more features than he will ever use in this lifetime or the next.
'Come on then Mr Condemned Man, let's grab a brew before we meet with the executioner. My treat.'

Fifteen minutes later we are standing outside Wilks' office like a couple of naughty schoolboys waiting for the headmaster. The offices here are better soundproofed than mine as we can only hear a muffled conversation from behind the door. It sounds heated. I shrug my shoulders at JD who grimaces and raises both eyebrows in a 'what can you do' manner. I knock on the frosted glass door and enter without waiting for a response.

'You wanted to see us Ma'am.'

Inside the Superintendent and the Commissioner stop their discussion immediately. He looks at us in the doorway and then back to her.

'Patricia, you know my thoughts on the matter. I will leave this with you.'

We both mumble 'Sir' as we move out of his way and let him pass. His face is not difficult to read, he is furious.

'Come in gentlemen, take a seat. JD, close the door behind you please.'

Shit, I think, this can't be good. I hate it when I'm right.

'Help me out here Peter. Why should we keep you on the team?'

The question is blunt and direct. My respect for Wilks goes up a notch. She has only been head of the Serious Crimes Unit for two months and this is the first real chance I have had of seeing her in action. It must have been tough taking over the role just at the time the biggest murder investigation in years is being undertaken and I realise she must be getting pressure from all sides to perform.

She continues, 'You must understand the difficult position this places me in. Places you in. We have a senior officer in charge of the highest profile case since God knows when and he is personally involved with a potential victim. I am sorry for your personal circumstances but we must ensure that the investigation is not compromised by an individual's actions. The press are already all over this trying to push a vigilante cop angle to it. We can't allow that to happen Peter, I'm sure you understand.'

JD gets to his feet, 'So it's already decided then is it. For Christs sake! You are about to remove the best detective you have on the Met from a case that needs all the help it can get to keep the momentum going. So his sister is a possible victim,' JD pauses, looks at me and his voice softens, 'I know that will only strengthen his resolve to continue this investigation to the best of his abilities. Compromise? There is nothing this man will do to compromise the safety of his sister or obtaining a conviction of whoever is behind this crime. You want to get this guy, we need Peter Carter on the team.'

'JD, sit down.' I say.

He suddenly realises he is standing up and gripping the edge of the desk fiercely. With his muscle power he is danger of ripping a large chunk of the wood off the side of the Superintendent's desk.

'Come on JD, we both know there's no choice in the matter for any of us. As soon as that reporter, what was his name, Soper? As soon as he asked that question about Helen, I was off the case. It is personal for me now, but ma'am, it always has been.' I turn to address Wilks, 'All cases are personal for me. Each and every body that turns up, each battered and bruised kid we have to scrape off the floor of some shitty room, each one, every one means something to me. Some officers get through the day by blocking out the victim, I can't do that. Every person we find is family to me. Every scumbag that causes harm I want to rip their throat out and leave them to die in the street but I know that justice is what really hurts these people. That is how I get through the day. That is why I do this job. Take me off this case as lead detective, put JD in my place, but don't throw me off it completely. I'm not going to beg but I will ask for you to consider my request.'

Wilks crosses her arms and I can see by the look on her face the personal dilemma she is facing.

'As you say DCI Carter, there is really no choice. The Commissioner and myself were having a similar discussion before you arrived, with much the same conclusion.'

Standing she turns and gazes out of the window across the London skyline.

'You are being relieved of this case by DI Dawkins. Congratulations JD, you have just made acting DCI for the duration of this investigation.'

There is a long pause as she continues to stare out of the window. JD looks like he is about to say something but I grab his arm and shake my head.

'You know Peter, when I started in this job, a woman was ridiculed by her colleagues. We were supposedly weaker, not up to the task, too likely to take things personally. Now things are better, the institutionalised sexism and racism is being eradicated but I still hear how we 'take things too personally'. I don't think that's a character flaw. I think that can be a strength and a show of pride.' She turns back to face us, 'The Commissioner wants you off the investigation completely and forced to take a leave of absence. I was defending you this morning. His response was to remind me about loyalty within the chain of command and how it affects careers.'

I think back to the conversation the Commissioner and I had that morning prior to the press conference.

'I am going to be loyal Peter. I want you to continue investigating this case but I want you out of the media spotlight and out of the Commissioner's gaze. I know you have a close working relationship with the Forensic Investigation Team so I want you to work from there as a liaison between the departments. If you are at the scene as part of a forensic team I want you suited and booted before you even set foot out of your vehicle. Mask, hood, the lot. I want you to be faceless but I want you there.

JD, are you OK with that as lead investigator? I don't want to stand on your toes.'

The smile from JD says it all, 'No ma'am that is absolutely peachy with me.'

'Peter, to all intents and purposes you are off the case according to this department. That will keep the Commissioner happy and we all know that is half the battle around here.'

The intensity of Wilks' gaze hits me.

'Peter, JD, this is personal to all of us. Let's catch this bastard before he causes any more damage.'

Her face softens, 'Now piss off and get it done. I'll deal with upstairs.'

I nod my thanks as we leave, no words need to be said. As we make our way back to my office I pull out my mobile phone.
'Doc, it's Peter. Do you have spare room in your office for a small desk and a big DCI?'
Even JD can hear the laughter down the phone as we make the arrangements to keep me working on the investigation. To keep me a part of the team that will find my sister.

CHAPTER 14

That afternoon I find myself standing behind Graham as he runs through the bite analysis procedure. I wanted to see how he could be so sure the facial bite marks on Claire Shannon, our latest victim, were from my sister. On screen is a high definition photograph of the bite marks from Claire's face. Graham points at the screen with a pen as he talks.
'As you can see, bite marks tend to have a double horseshoe shaped pattern. This layer of marks is caused by the six teeth of the upper jaw and this layer by the six teeth of the lower jaw. Now bite marks in flesh tend to be less defined than those found in food due to the flexible nature of skin. But when the skin is necrotised it can be clearer to see as is the case here.'
'You're telling me Helen bit this woman when she was dead?'
'It would appear to be the case and it would also appear it was done with deliberate force to create the patterns you see.'
I look at the image more carefully. There are three bite marks on the cheeks, all distinct. I wonder what would cause Helen to do such a thing, and as I do so, Graham continues his lesson in bite analysis.
'There was no struggle during the bite process, notice the clear, defined edges. Also note how you can see the ridges between the teeth…' he zooms in onto one of the right cheeks bite marks, '…here and here. We can even discern a chipped tooth pattern here which corresponds to Helen's most recent dental examination.'
From his desk he produces an X-ray of a jaw with my sister's name written in careful block capitals at the top and places it next to the keyboard.

'We use this piece of software to scan in the x-ray and the dental impressions and turn it into a 3D model. It really is very good, it was developed by the Forensic Odontology Department at the University of Granada in Spain. A friend of mine sent it over for me to try out and I am very impressed by the results.'

Graham clicks a few icons on the screen and a rendered 3D model appears, rotating about its axis showing the full dental details from all angles. He clicks again and we zoom into the upper jaw and the top front tooth.

'See the chipping of the enamel here. This compares with the bite mark...' another click of the mouse and the photograph of the cheek is superimposed onto the 3D model. It matches perfectly, '...here.'

He turns to look at me, 'Every persons dental imprints are unique, like fingerprints, but harder to obtain. Tooth enamel is the hardest tissue in the body, so it is difficult for a person to change their dental print without performing severe damage to the teeth. Even after an extreme temperature fire when bone has turned to dust we find teeth amongst the ashes. Forensically we can determine quite accurately age, sex and even occupation from a persons teeth after death. If we have the records of a person ante-mortem it is a simple case of matching the two together to perform a 99% accurate identification.'

I look incredulous, 'How can a persons teeth prove their occupation? You're pulling my leg right?'

Graham leans back in his chair.

'Construction workers have more scratches on the enamel of their teeth due to the cement dust environment they work in. The same is true for bakers with flour dust. Another example is that a carpenter may have small grooves in the upper and lower teeth where nails are placed in the mouth prior to hammering into the wood. We used to see discolouration from ink in office workers, from the pen sucking, but now that has changed due to everyone using computers. We still see discolouration in jewellers and watchmakers from the precious metals used in these environments. It's not an exact science but we can make a best guess as to a person's job.'
'Unbelievable.' I mutter.
Graham brings up the other two bite patterns and overlays the 3D model on each. Each one matches perfectly with Helen's 3D model.
'Normally we need a minimum of four or five teeth to create a match. Helen has managed to provide us with a minimum of four teeth impressions on this one and ten usable imprints on this bite, the last bite.'
'Sorry to butt in Doc, but how do you know that's the last bite?'
'The first bite, whilst firm was tentative. It is like she didn't really want to do it. As she grows used to the process the bites are firmer. The first bite is like a nip of the front teeth, like putting something in your mouth you don't want to. The second bite is more substantial but the last bite has ten defined teeth marks and two that would normally be dismissed as evidence due to the soft edges. Peter, I can only assume Helen knew what she was doing when she made these marks. She was telling us she is still alive.'

I think of Helen biting down on a dead woman's flesh in desperation to be identified, to be helped. I realise my sister is stronger, both physically and mentally, than I have ever imagined.

'Is there any indication when the bites were made? How long ago? Any clue as to Helen's location?'

'As with the other victims, the body parts have been washed and scrubbed thoroughly to remove any evidence then placed in a cool sterile environment, and that also makes time of death difficult to determine. However there is a trace element of saliva with these bite marks. It doesn't give us TOD but due to the breakdown of enzymes in the saliva we can estimate that the bite occurred sometime within the last 36 hours. It gives us hope that Helen is still alive Peter.'

'But time is running out Doc. Time is running out for us all.' I want to be out on the streets banging down doors, searching, doing something to help the investigation along. I just have to trust JD and the department with that process, the Commissioner has seen to that. I am lost in my thoughts as Graham starts talking again, I miss the first few words.

'...location near the Thames is probable.'

I snap my head around, 'What was that Doc, say that again.'

'You asked about location, in the autopsy we found traces of what can only be described as mist droplets of river water attached to the saliva. We deduced that a location near the Thames is probable but we are waiting on the full results of that analysis to return from the labs in Oxford. It should be completed by tomorrow morning. It's all in the report we sent to your office...' He trails off, realising it is no longer my office.

The ringing of my cell phone hides his embarrassment and my feelings of helplessness.

'Carter.' I answer brusquely without even looking at the display.

Julia, my girlfriend, is crying down the phone line.

'Peter, it's my father, he's in the hospital. Someone almost killed him at the restaurant this morning. Please I need you to help him, help us.' She sobs loudly, 'Please Peter, help me.'

CHAPTER 15

'He has suffered a crushed right orbital eye socket, multiple facial fractures, a broken left arm, three broken ribs and brain injuries from a severe concussion. The paramedics had to perform an emergency intercostal drain due to a tension pneumothorax caused by a rib puncturing his lung. There were three fingers on his left hand we were unable to reattach, but he should retain mobility in the hand.'

I am with Julia at the Royal London Hospital as she sobs softly at the bedside of her father and my friend, Nektarios. He is in the High Dependency Unit and hidden behind a swathe of bandages and tubes. The soft beeping of a monitor in the background is strangely reassuring.

'To be honest, I have not seen injuries like these where the patient was still alive at the scene. We have him in an induced coma so we can monitor his brain function and give his body a chance to recover from the battering he has received.'

The surgeon focuses on Julia and holds her hand, woman to woman.

'Your father is a strong man. He has a hard struggle ahead but he is in the best hands with my team. We will do all we can to get him through this and bring him back to you. The first 48 hours are critical, his strength has got him through the initial stages but now we are here to help him.'

'Will he live?' Julia manages to ask.

'I won't lie to you. He has sustained massive trauma that a body should not be able to withstand. At the moment I give his chances at greater than 50%. I am sorry, but I want you to be prepared should the worst happen. Have you any other family members who you need to contact? It would be best if they know sooner rather than later.'

Julia nods. 'My mother is home in Greece visiting my sister and her grandchildren.'
She turns to me.
'Peter, can you help me speak to them? I'm not sure I can do it alone.'
I nod and kiss her forehead.
'Anything you want me to do, I'm there for you. I'm there for all of you.'
In the background the beeping continues its unmelodic song of a man's struggle for survival.
'There is nothing we can do here, what about I take you home and we call your family from my place. If there is a change in your father's condition my place is only ten minutes away, we can back here in no time.'
The Dr backs me up, 'That's a good idea. All we can do at the moment is wait and monitor your father. Go home, contact your family and try and get some rest.'
I give her my business card, 'This is where we will be. Please call if there is any change.'
She glances briefly at the card and I see her expression change as she sees my job title and the Homicide and Serious Crime Command logo.
'We will call you immediately, don't worry.'
She hugs Julia and says her goodbyes to me and we slowly walk away from the HDU, make our way to my car and I drive back to my apartment in silence. Julia stares out of the window for the duration of the ten minute drive, her thoughts elsewhere. I don't press her or try to make conversation. I have been around enough victims' relatives to know that sometimes they need to process the horror of what's happened before being able to move forward.

My apartment at Barrier Point belongs to my brother Paul and Katarina, my sister-in-law. Before they were married and moved to Crete she worked as a communications manager for a large media company in the city. She bought the place while it was still off plan and got it at a very good price before the property prices went crazy. When she and Paul had their first child she gave up work to concentrate on bringing up Ethan. It was when my second nephew, Thomas, was born that they started planning their move to Crete nearer Katarina's family. On the day Paul left the army last year they moved. Luckily for me the property bubble was well and truly burst, so instead of selling up the apartment they rent it to me at a minimum rate. As Paul pointed out, it's better to have someone in it looking after the place. When they come back for a week each year, I move out into a hotel and they have their place back. It's a small price to pay for such a fantastic apartment. I have thought about asking to buy it from them at some point but I never seem to get around to it in our brief monthly phone calls.

I wave to the concierge as I park the car in the underground car park. As I get out of the car he walks out of his office with a large parcel.

'Mr Carter, I have another package for you sir. Looks like it's from your brother again.'

He sees Julia getting out of the car and her obvious distress as he hands the parcel over to me.

'Oh…is everything all right? Can I do anything to help?' The questions are directed towards me. He finds it hard to talk to Julia, I think it is because he has a soft spot for her.

'Just some bad news Harry. We'll be fine. Thanks for this.' I raise the parcel towards him in acknowledgement.

I hold Julia's hand as we make our way up to the apartment. Luckily the lifts are working again because I hate the walk up the 12 flights of stairs when the 'Out Of Order' signs are on display.

I have to release her hand as I open the front door and she leans into my arm, holding on with both hands. I walk through the small hallway, through the living room where I set my parcel down on the dining table before opening the patio doors to the balcony. Julia sits herself down at the large dining table, places her head in her hands and begins to cry. 'Oh Peter, I just feel so helpless. Seeing him like that it's..' She doesn't manage any more words as heart breaking sobs erupt from her slight frame. I go to her and do all I can at a time like this. I kneel before her, hold her in my arms and tell her everything will be alright. They are words I am not sure even I believe at this moment in time.

One hour later we have explained the situation to Julia's mother and Nektarios' brothers, Stelios and Babis. We have booked them on an Aegean Airlines flight from Chania to Gatwick with a 5 hour changeover in Athens. I had forgotten that during the winter months there are no direct flights to, or from, Crete. They arrive tomorrow at 9pm and I said we would be there to pick them up. The rapid fire Greek conversation between Julia and her family sounded so heated at one point I had to ask what was going on. Julia actually managed a smile when she turned to me and whispered, 'Uncle Babis wants to bring his shotgun and hunt down the man who did this. I am trying to persuade him that it will not be possible.' She shrugs her shoulders in that Greek way and says 'Sfakians.'
I have no idea what that means but I have to admit that I am looking forward to meeting her family.

CHAPTER 16

Helen is disgusted and ashamed to realise she is approaching orgasm. Her breath is coming in shallow gasps through the tight-fitting leather hood they always make her put on before she is taken from the room. She tells herself it is because she is getting used to the treatment they are inflicting on her. Her mind is screaming out 'NO' as she is abused but her body rebels against her thoughts and another wave of pleasure courses through her.
The man behind her is thrusting himself into her frenziedly now as he approaches his own climax. She cannot help herself as she moans through the leather face mask and feels him pound into her sensitive flesh. He stiffens and grips her tightly as he comes. As she feels her body turn to liquid fire and explode around him a foot crashes into her side, instantly turning her pleasure into cruel pain. It is accompanied by a guttural, brutal laugh.
'My turn. Get off her, I'll show the bitch how to moan properly.'
The man on top of her is pushed off and she is roughly turned over. As he enters her he punches and kneads her body with a brutal force. Helen's muffled moans continue while her body is used by this other man, but this time it is not from pleasure, but pain.

Zoe hears what is happening but cannot see anything as she also has been restricted by a tight leather hood. She followed Helen's lead when the black objects were thrown into the room after hearing what would happen if she did not put one of them on. She has been tied to two sturdy chairs with her legs spread wide apart and just open space beneath her body. Her arms have been stretched out wide either side of her with her wrists tied to secure points in the wall. Her thighs and calves are screaming out in pain as she tries to support her body weight and she is trembling from the effort. She feels doubly naked with the way her legs have been spread so wide, exposed to whoever is watching her. She couldn't help herself but she has voided her bowels through fear and shame. The only response was a laugh from one of the men. She has not been touched yet, but she is waiting in terror for the men to come to her. The smell of leather, old sweat and fear from the inside of the hood is cloying. The sounds of abuse from the room, the smell of her own stench, plus the fear that she is next for the men's attention is too much for her and she starts to feel nauseous. The vomit rushes from her mouth without anywhere for it to escape and she begins to gag. Panic sets in as she struggles to breathe. Zoe is trying to breathe through her nose but the vomit has spread inside the mask and is blocking her nostrils. The holes for her mouth and nose are blocked now. She can feel vomit dripping down her body through the breathing holes and from beneath the neck line, but too slowly to allow any respite from the suffocating semi liquid. She starts to thrash uncontrollably against the restraints as she starts to choke to death.
'Stop the fucking camera!'

Helen is pushed roughly to one side and collapses on to the floor as the man behind her shouts the command to his companion. She cannot do anything but lie there, naked, and allow the pain to flow through her body. She is dimly aware of voices around her.

'Get the mask off.'
'Is the camera off?'
'Is she dead?'
'IS THE FUCKING CAMERA OFF?'
A pause, 'Camera is off, get her mask off.'
There is a sound of things being scraped across the hard floor and then Helen feels something warm, wet and heavy slap against her breasts. Zoe's facemask, she thinks numbly.
'Turn her on her side, sweep her mouth out. We have to clear her airway'
Choking noises echo around the room followed by a heavy sigh of relief.
'Jesus that was close. Bloody hell Jim she could have died and you're bothered about the camera.'
'I told you not to say my name.'
'You said not to use it when the cameras are filming. What's your problem? Don't you ever tell the girls your name or something. You don't want them to go back to your wife and tell them your dirty little secret, that you like to use whores is that it? For crying out loud, they're hookers who know what they're getting into, it's not like they will show up on your doorstep in…'
'SHUT THE FUCK UP. Just don't say another fucking word or I swear I will…'
'What…you swear what. Beat me like you like to do with them. Bollocks to this. No more for me. It's been fun, but you are getting beyond a joke. You can't control yourself. One of these days you are going to kill one of these girls and I can't believe one of them hasn't reported you yet. I know I pay a lot to do this, but fuck me, watching you do what you do is not worth it. I don't care how much we make on the net. I'm through.'

ONE PIECE AT A TIME

The words sink into Helen's brain like a spoon through thick custard. The younger sounding man doesn't know the truth. He doesn't know about the other girls, their deaths. She wants to scream but all she can manage is a moan through the face mask. She strives to form words but the mask is too tight against her lips, the air holes too small. Help me, please help me she says, but all that comes out is,
'Elf ee lee self ee'
Even Helen can't understand herself and all she earns as a result is a kick to the back of her thigh. The pain explodes in her leg and she screams through the mask.
'Shut up bitch.'
'Jim, stop, you fucking psycho. I'm taking this one to a hospital to check her out and I'm going to take her to wherever she wants to go.'
A gentle hand is placed under her shoulder and starts to help her from the floor. She stands on shaky legs.
'Come on, lets get this mask off you and then we'll get both your clothes and get you and your friend out of here.'
The ties at the back of the mask are released and Helen can breathe fully once more. She turns to look at the man who is holding her,
'Help me. Help me please.'
Tears start to stream down her face.
'I will. I will get you out of here and your friend too. Where are your clothes?'
Helen is groggy from pain and can only look quizzically at this man before her.
'I don't know. He took them, he...' she starts to nod her head in the direction of the other man just in time to see the knife blade flashing towards her.
She manages to scream out a choked 'NO' and raise her right arm in defence, but the knife flashes past her and streaks towards her would be saviour.

As the knife plunges into the younger man's neck she sees his sudden look of comprehension as he realises fatally what he has been a part of. Blood sprays across her face and she gags on the hot, coppery taste of it. His mouth opens and closes but no sounds emerge as he releases his grip on her arms and turns to face his attacker. His blood is pumping out fiercely with every beat of his heart, spraying the room and his attacker. His knees buckle as he looks to them both for help, his hands trying to close the gaping wound in his neck. He looks Helen straight in the eyes. She wants to think his mouth is forming words. She wants to think he is struggling to say sorry but all that can be heard is a disturbing gurgle. He completes the strange choreography of his death by slowly slumping to the floor, never taking his eyes off Helen's. Then he is gone, like a candle being blown out in the wind, his eyes lose their life and he is still. Helen cannot take her eyes off the fixed gaze of the dead man in front of her. After a minute of standing there looking at him, jumbled thoughts running through her head, she nods her head towards the body, 'You want me to chop him up as well?'

CHAPTER 17

I stayed up most of the night with Julia at my apartment. We opened the parcel from my brother together and she started crying when she saw the five litre can of olive oil. I learned so much about her and her family, so much about her father and his beloved island of Crete and why he moved here and made a new start in London. I let her talk until she ran out of words to say and then I held her in my arms and made promises that I cannot keep about everything being alright.

I share with her the secrets of my childhood and the struggles of staying close to a sister I never saw apart from a few hours a week. I tell her the problems Helen has faced and overcome and how strong she is. It is Julia's turn to hold me then and give me promises I know no-one can keep.

We both try to sleep but lie there in my bed holding hands, waiting for the phone to ring. I curse when it is my mobile phone that breaks the silence of pre-dawn. Julia sits bolt upright, a look of terror on her face, thinking it is a call from the hospital. I look at the display and shake my head.

'JD' I say.

I get out of bed and pad through to the kitchen before pressing the Accept button. I figure whatever the call is about, I am going to need a strong cup of coffee to revitalise my senses.

'Peter, are you near your computer?'

'Morning JD, give me a minute to turn it on. What's going on? We have a lead?'

I pick out a plain white mug and set it on the counter in front of the kettle.

'We have video of the guy. Video of him with women.'

I forget the coffee and switch off the kettle.

'I'm coming in.'

'I'm in the cyber crime unit, come straight there Peter. We are gonna catch this creep. See you soon.'

He hangs up and I walk swiftly through the apartment to the bedroom to let Julia know I have to go. She has already fallen back asleep so I write a brief note to tell her I will be with her if she needs me. I leave the apartment quietly and a half hour later I am in the air conditioned office space of the CCU, the Met's Cyber Crime Unit.

JD knows my needs so well as he hands me a stainless steel travel mug of the most wonderful smelling coffee.

'Here, thought you might need this. How's Julia and her father.'

My grimace and so-so gesture says it all.

'Sorry Peter, I have heard there is progress in the case, but they won't go into details with me just yet. You know what they can be like sometimes, afraid we will nick the case off them when they have done all the hard work. They can't understand we are all on the same side.'

The 'they' he is talking about are the City of London Police, a separate entity to the Met and sometimes there can be friction between the two departments.

'So what do we have on our guy? CCTV footage?'

JD leans across the young man in front of him and hands me a sheet of paper full of lists of numbers.

'Bring it up Luke.'

The young man types away at the keyboard and hits enter with a flourish. I notice that even in the controlled environment room he is sweating.

'Do you mind if I go and get a cup of tea, I just don't want to sit through this again.'

JD nods his approval and sympathetically says,

'No problem, we'll come and get you when we need you.'

I look at the screen in front of me and the website that is displayed there. Pictures of naked women chained to walls adorn either side of the web page. Their identity is hidden by a black mask. Blood red letters stand out against the dark back ground asking for a password to enter for 'The Forbidden Pleasures' or to use a credit card to gain access.
'This site was brought to our attention yesterday by the Operation Yewtree guys after one of them thought he recognised our photo-fit subject. They have been monitoring this for a while because they have found it on the computers of a few of their suspects.'
JD pulls over a chair for me and we both sit down. I sip my coffee as he continues, computer crime is not my forte and I don't want to stop him with questions just yet.
'It's a securely encrypted site, which is nothing special these days. What makes this stand out is it using a layer of encryption developed by the US Naval Research Lab to effectively hide the source of the web site.'
He sees the look of confusion on my face.
'You're wondering how this program is being used by someone not from the Naval Research Lab right? Well they made it open source, meaning they gave it away for free so that people in countries with, shall we say, not he best human rights records, can safely send information of their governments activities around the web. It hides users identification and web locations by routing their traffic through hundreds, if not thousands, of layers of separately encrypted net identifiers. It is virtually impossible to crack.'
'What about credit card payments, you have to be able to trace those right.'
'It used to be simple, but now,' he clicks on the Credit Card icon and a new web page appears, 'now they use bitcoins to pay for things.'
Putting my coffee down, I look at the screen.
'What the bloody hell is a bitcoin?'

JD snorts derisively, 'Only the biggest scheme of money laundering out there. You want to send £100,000 of your hard earned drug money in London to New York, you get five of your friends to each deposit £20K into a Western Union account. No problem we can trace that. What then happens is you convert all five accounts into bitcoins at a local internet café, completely anonymously and you don't even pay any commission. These bitcoins are then cashed out or spent on whatever you want on the internet. Cashing out is completely secure and can be done anonymously with a username and password from an account you set up that morning. You don't need ID, you don't need an address, you do pay for cashing out but it's a paltry amount when you look at it. Worst thing about it all is that it is all completely legal. There is not a thing we can do about it and we can't trace the guys moving millions across international borders at the click of a mouse.'

'So we can't trace the location of the site, we don't have a name, and we can't trace the money. What the hell am I doing here JD? You said you had video of our guy. Where is it and what is this?' I wave the papers in front of me.

'The numbers are our tech guys, the geeks, trying to trace back to the source of the website and the source of these videos.'

JD winces as he leans forward in his seat and types something into the computer.

'It's not pretty Peter. Luke has had to watch this three or four times already, that's why he wanted to leave.'

He moves the mouse over a small icon of a woman being impaled on a stake.

'Here we go.'

JD clicks the left mouse button and a video starts to play on the screen.

Forty minutes later I am once again shocked by the inhumanity we as the human race manage to achieve on a regular basis. I try not to think that one of those poor women in the videos could be my sister.

JD has just paused the last video and zoomed in to the top left corner of the screen. There is a boarded up window there. 'The glass here gives us a reflective surface, see the red light of the camera just here.' He points to the screen. He drops his hand to the desk top and starts playing around with the mouse opening a new program.

'This was enhanced by the Yewtree gang.'

Another mouse click. I stare at the screen and cannot take my eyes away from the face of our 'man of interest. He is standing behind a tripod with a small video camera placed upon it. His features are contorted into a grimace of ecstasy as he watches the unfolding scene of torture and rape in front of him. Everything up until this point has included figures in masks, both male and female, torturer and victims.

'This has now been distributed along with the photofit to all units around the UK. We are getting closer to this guy and his gang. We are working on the assumption that there are two maybe three men involved in this website. Peter, we have possibly three killers out there working as an organised group. We are looking at the website as inextricably linked to our investigation. The site opened two weeks before we found our first body and we have the same number of victims as women in this video. There are also links here that we have not yet managed to open. The encryption algorithms are defeating even our best geeks and their computing power. These could be more victims, but Luke seems to think that one of the links is from a live webcam. A live camera streaming constant video to whoever holds the key to unlock it.'

I look at JD, 'We need that video JD and we need it yesterday.' I stare back at the frozen picture on the screen with a chill of expectation running through my veins. I will find you, the only thought in my mind.

I will find you.

CHAPTER 18

I leave JD with the IT geeks trying to figure out how to crack the encryption on the live video feed and make my way over to Graham's office. My temporary office whilst this investigation continues. He is already there, working feverishly away at his computer. The smell of fresh Jamaican Blue Mountain emanates from the coffee machine in the corner of the large office. I walk towards it to get my second fix of the day and pour the hot black liquid into a mug adorned with skulls. Sometimes, I think, Graham can be a little weird.

'How come you have the largest office of anyone I know who works at the Met?'

His head pops up from behind his monitor like a computer literate meerkat.

'What was that?'

'I said, how come you have the largest office in the Met. Even the Commissioner's office is smaller than this one.'

'You know, Peter, that's your fault. When you enquired about getting me down here I just made a few stipulations. One was floor space. I love having the room to move around, it helps me think. It's also great for parties.'

I look at him over the top of my skull mug. He can't hold his poker face for long and starts to laugh.

'It's actually an old store room. When I first arrived I was given that tiny little office next to the cold room, you know, the morgue. Anyway, I found this place half empty so I had a word with Shirley at HR and she OK'd the move. A lick of paint, a new desk, the IT department installed the new ports, flushed the taps and here I am.'

'I get the paint and desk but ports and taps, you lost me there.'

Graham has a little chuckle at me.

'You really are a dinosaur. Don't worry, we'll get you into the 21st century before you know it.'
His expression turns serious, 'How's the father-in-law to be?'
I shake my head and ignore the father-in-law jibe.
'Not good. Not good at all. The surgeon, well she gave him a greater than 50% chance, but he's strong and he's got the heart of an ox. If anyone can pull through he can.'
Graham ignores his computer work for a moment.
'Any news on what happened to him, who did it, motive?'
I shake my head again.
'They're going through his security tapes but whoever did this had wiped the recordings for yesterday. The tech guys, JD calls them geeks, are trying to restore them but they are not too hopeful about it. They say it's been completely trashed.'
'Hmmm. Let's hope he can tell us something when he wakes up. Be positive about that.'
The phone in my pocket interrupts our conversation. The caller ID shows 'The Boss'.
I roll my eyes at Graham and hit the accept button.
'Good morning Superintendent. What can I do for you?'
It is not a pleasant tone that greets me down the line.
'What were you doing at the cyber crime unit this morning? I told you to stay out of the way and out of the Commissioner's line of fire. He has already had me in his office for a grilling about why you were looking at information regarding the Ripper case.'
'Ma'am, I was there to ask personally about getting my ports flushed for a tap in Dr Young's office. It was a complete coincidence that…'
'Don't bullshit me Carter, you can't tell a port from a bloody USB connection,' a laugh and a pause 'but it will be good enough for the Commissioner. What did you find out?'

'Sorry boss, it won't happen again. They have a workable picture that is already doing the rounds. It is more than a mere similarity of the photofit. It's bloody identical. They are also chasing up a lead about a live video stream. They seem to think if they can find a way to crack that they can give us a location.'

'Any views on a location yet?'

'Not yet, but we do think it may be near the river somewhere. Dr Young is waiting on the analysis of residue found on the last victim that showed evidence of water droplets or mist that bear all the characteristics of river water.'

Graham picks up the phone and mouths 'On it' to me.

'He is chasing that up as we speak ma'am.'

'Good, keep me informed and keep a bloody low profile from now on. I haven't got a clue how the Commissioner found out about this morning, perhaps someone is gunning for you. Watch your back and stay low. And Peter, sorry to hear about your girlfriend's father, I'm sure the City force are all over it. What with that and Helen…well I'm sorry. Perhaps it would be best if you take the rest of the day and go to Julia. That's not a request Peter. The investigation will continue without you for one day and I believe you need time to come to terms with everything. Come back tomorrow with your batteries recharged. Take the day to be with someone you care about, let her take care of you as you take of her.'

I mumble my thanks as she hangs up and wonder how everyone knows my personal life so well.

'Peter, the results are on their way over but it's not good news I'm afraid. All they will say is that the results are inconclusive. Incon-bloody-clusive, bane of my life that word. What it means is someone hasn't got the balls to back up their work.'

I am still standing there, coffee in one hand and phone in the other as I pursue avenues in my train of thought about Helen, the Ripper case, Julia, Nektarios and someone from within the force out to get me.

Graham chuckles, not noticing my dazed look, 'Flush the ports and get a tap, you almost had it then.'
I smile weakly, put my phone away and take a sip of the coffee.
'Do you think you could take a look at the report and read between the lines? See what you can come up with and inform JD of the findings. I've been ordered to take a day's leave of absence. Recharge my batteries as she put it.'
All of a sudden I feel weary beyond belief, not just my body, but my mind as well. It must be obvious as Graham looks at me and says with compassion his voice,
'Peter, go home. Be with Julia and her father. We'll see you tomorrow. We've got this.'

I don't remember the journey home from the office. Julia is up and sits with a mug of hot tea on the terrace in the feeble warmth of the February sun. The steam is rising from her mug and curling and drifting around her face as she sips the hot sweet tea. I drag the seat that is opposite her closer so our knees are touching when I sit down. I place my hands on her knees and look into her beautiful brown eyes.
'Julia, will you marry me?'

CHAPTER 19

It is only as Richard steps into his office he realises that he has not heard from Zoe in the last twenty four hours and she has still not turned up for work. Trying her number again only returns the same answerphone message as yesterday. He walks across to Martin's office and enters the open doorway. Martin is on the telephone and holds up a hand with his index finger raised in the universal sign language for 'one second'. Richard waits uncomfortably for him to finish his phone call. 'OK, no problem. You'll have them first thing this afternoon…yes…yes..OK. They will be in your inbox by midday…Right…bye.' Martin puts down the phone and waves Richard over, 'Bloody Head Office, always wanting sales reports. Yes Richard, what can I do for you?'
He walks over to the small desk, cluttered with pens, reams of paper and photographs of Martin's family.
'It's Zoe. She still hasn't got back to me and she's not in work again today. After what you said yesterday about the missing girls…well frankly I'm worried about her. I know she's only been here a few months but this isn't like her. Should we inform the police or something?'
Martin places his elbows on the desk and steeples his fingers in front of his face. He regards this as his intelligent pose, when he needs time to think. It allows him time to process. 'Hmmm. What about her family? Surely it should be up to them to report her missing don't you think? Try and see if any of them know anything about her not turning up for work. I agree Richard, it is worrying, but I don't want to appear melodramatic and give the police more work when they already have so much on their plate. Try her mother, I'm sure there will be a number on her file somewhere. Let me know how you get on with that and then we'll decide a further course of action.'

Richard nods his agreement.

'I suppose you're right. Sorry about that, just feeling a bit twitchy with the news going on and on about the Ripper. I'll see what her mum has to say. Do you need help with the sales figures?'

Martin shakes his head,

'No…no, I got it. No need to worry about that.'

Martin tries not to show panic in his voice, he doesn't want Richard anywhere near the sales figures. He smiles,

'I'll collate the info and get it off to head office straight away.'

As Richard leaves his office Martin wonders how he is going to manage this month in explaining the deficit between stock levels and sales figures. His little ebay business selling IT equipment may have to be curtailed for a while or someone will put two and two together and cry thief.

Richard sits down at his desk, too pre-occupied with Zoe to notice Martin's panic. He calls up the personnel files for Zoe Walker on the staff roster spreadsheet and takes note of the emergency contact number she gave during her application. The phone is answered after two rings,

'Hello, is that Mrs Temple? Hello. My name is Richard Barnwell, I am Zoe's manager at Staples. Is she available for me to have a word with her please.'

The negative response from Zoe's mother is like a lead ball in his gut.

'I see. Can you tell me when you last spoke to Zoe because we haven't seen her at work since the day before yesterday.'

Richard doesn't expect the tirade of abuse that expels itself down the telephone.

'OK, Mrs Temple,' he hastily says, 'We'll let you know if we hear from her too.'

He hangs up before she can continue.

'Like mother like daughter,' he whispers under his breath.

He calls Martin on the internal number.

'Martin, hi. Zoe's mother hasn't seen her in over a month and went on about Zoe owing her money amongst other things, so not much help there. I think we ought to inform the police. It seems prudent with the goings on at the moment to (pause)…yes (pause)…no (pause, longer this time)…Martin I…OK…OK. I'll wait another twenty four hours as you say. Sorry to bother you.'
Richard hangs up the phone but cannot shake the feeling that something is wrong.
'Fuck it,' he mutters and picks up the phone again as he dials a set of numbers.
'Hello. I'd like to report a missing person please.'
As he says these words Richard feels the weight lift from his shoulders.

CHAPTER 20

JD is really hoping for a breakthrough with the internet encryption. If they could just crack the trail of servers and clients that the video feed is being processed through they could pinpoint a physical location of the web camera streaming the video. He thought he knew his way around a computer system, but watching Luke at the keyboard is like watching the performance of a maestro at a piano. Unfortunately this performance seems to be hitting all the wrong notes.
'Damn it!' Luke spits out as yet another attempt to trace the signal routing fails.
'There's no way we can crack this. The NSA in the States can't manage it so why do we think we can do any better.'
JD crosses his arms, a grim look on his face.
'What if we are trying to do this the wrong way.'
Luke looks around,
'What do you mean?'
JD strokes his chin in thought,
'What if we are looking for the trace in the wrong place? Would all the subscribers have to use this TOR to watch the stream?'
Luke shakes his head as a smile appears on his face and says simply, 'No.'
JD slaps him on the back.
'Lets get to work on seeing which freaks have signed up to this without setting up the encryption,' Luke's hands are already flying across the keyboard, 'and then we'll pay them a visit and see what happens from there.'

'Sir, if we can find someone who is online, subscribed and has established a connection to this stream then we are ninety per cent of the way there. All we need to do then is track the routing from one machine to another. We have software that can handle that. I designed it myself.'
The muscular detective's eyes rise in surprise and astonishment at this revelation.
'How come you're not out there earning millions with some dot com company if you can write software like that?'
Without even turning from the screen Luke replies,
'I was caught hacking into the Met's servers to try and remove some parking fines for a friend of mine. I got through the first levels of security no problem and then came up against a brick wall. Took me a few hours to sort that out, but what I didn't realise was that it was all a sham. A dummy server to expose people like me and stop the chancers. The ones that manage to get through the last security protocols, and there have only been two in the last four years, are given a choice. I say choice but it was more of an ultimatum. The woman who interviewed me said I could go to University to study Computer Forensic Science, have all my tuition paid for in return for a five year term of service with the Met. Or, this is where the choice comes in, she could always provide me with a short custodial sentence and the threat of having someone watching everything I do for the rest of my life.'
A string of numbers appear on the monitor in front of him. Luke points to a seemingly random sequence of numbers and letters.
'Gotcha.'
'What are we looking at here Luke?'
The tension and excitement in JD's voice is all too apparent.
'That, sir, that, is an e-mail address of a subscriber to the site along with an E-mail address of the host.'
'E-mail? How is that going to help us?'
The fingers are typing furiously away and the printer starts churning out pages.

'Sir, these numbers are IP addresses and even better MAC addresses for the computers involved. All I need to do now is cross reference these identifiers with any e-commerce sites, you know Paypal, Google Checkout, even Amazon or ebay, and if they have been used by the host's machine we will have a name, address and even an inside leg measurement if you want it.'

JD punches the air and pulls out his mobile phone to dial Peter's number.

'How long will it take?'

Luke screws up his face.

'Ummm…that's the bad part. I will have to run it by the ITSSO for approval and she can be a right bitch at the best of times. The approval normally takes twelve hours to come through before I can start processing aggressively. Once I get that go ahead we should start to see results in twenty four to forty eight hours.'

Holding his phone out to Luke, JD says flatly,

'Whoever the IT Security Specialist Officer is, get them on the phone now and get them down here for a meeting with me. No bloody excuses.'

Luke reaches over to the desk phone sitting near the computer screen.

'No signal in here sir, we're in a Faraday cage, but it's no problem, I have the number on speed dial. She's the one who got me into this in the first place.'

He punches a key on the telephone.

'Morning Ma'am. I have a request from DI Dawkins for you.' A pause, 'Certainly, I'll pass him over.'

He hands the phone to JD, 'The ITSSO, Superintendent Wilks, for you sir.'

JD sighs and thinks why didn't I know it was her?

'Ma'am, we have a breakthrough in the Ripper case. We need a warrant pushing through to…' JD nods at the discussion taking place in his ear, 'Yes ma'am. Thank you. I will keep you informed.'

He hands the phone back to Luke so that it can be placed back in its cradle.

'She says do it.'

Luke smiles and starts hammering instructions onto the screen before him.

'It's going to be a long day sir. Any chance you can get me a brew?'

As JD walks away from the young man he can't help but mutter out loud with a hint of admiration in his voice, 'Cocky bastard.'

Once outside the room he tries to contact Peter on his mobile but only gets the DCI's voice-mail. He leaves a message asking Peter to call him back as he won't leave any other details over an unsecure line. He knows only too well the amount of information that can be obtained over mobile phones.

People look at him strangely as he walks through the corridors but he takes no notice of them. His thoughts are firmly on tracing and tracking down their killer before he can murder again, before he will murder again.

CHAPTER 21

Neal Stephens is back at the alley near Valascos Bakery. He is dressed slightly differently on this visit than his last time here. He is wearing a Hackett Mayfair Wool Mohair dark suit coupled with a light blue shirt and a black and red striped tie. His black Loake brogues and Prince of Wales check holdall top off the appearance of a well to do weekend traveller about the city. His face is clean shaven and he is almost unrecognisable as the man he was two days ago.
He takes a mobile phone from his pocket and dials a number.
'I'm here. Where do you want it placed?'
As he is listening to the instructions on the phone he bends down and opens the zip on the holdall. Placing his spare hand inside he brings out an object about the size of a hardback book. He walks over to a green dumpster on the left hand side of the alleyway and places the object underneath it.
'Done. Give me five minutes and then make the call. I'll see you back at the office in an hour or two. I will finish my side of things shortly, I want to see how they handle this.'
He shakes his head impatiently.
'No, make the call now. I'm on my way.'
He ends the conversation, places the phone back in his suit jacket pocket and nonchalantly walks out of the alleyway, under the 'Police Crime Scene' tape and heads towards the river.

He slowly strolls along like a man without a care in the world and stops a few hundred metres down the road at a Starbucks. He orders an Americano which he takes to a table for two by the window. He sits in one of the soft chairs, places the holdall on the other and takes a Blackberry from it. The message body and the recipient list has already been populated, all he has to do is hit send. He re-reads the short sentence in front of him.
'The end game has begun.'
He presses send with his thumb just as two police cars speed past the window, lights flashing and sirens wailing, towards the bakery.
Neal Stephens smiles to himself as he takes a careful sip of his hot, black coffee and watches the police arrive in force.

JD arrives on the scene just ten minutes after the first two squad cars screeched to a halt outside Valascos Bakery. Already there is a road block in place and the blue and white marker tape is out in abundance. He thinks about calling Peter but decides against it as he knows the Commissioner will blow a gasket if he finds out, and he seems to have eyes and ears everywhere. He finds it hard to believe that Peter thinks someone is trying to sabotage him but he finds it harder to believe that Peter and Julia are getting married. When Peter called him two hours ago and asked if he would be best man at his and Julia's wedding he actually burst out laughing and asked if Peter was serious. When Peter joined in the laughter and said he was 'deadly serious' and would he do it, JD agreed straight away.
He had let Peter know in that call about the potential breakthrough in the case and told him there would be no real progress until Luke had managed to back track through the e-commerce lists and come up with a match. JD promised to keep Peter informed and told him to make the most of the day off with his new fiancée.

ONE PIECE AT A TIME

Graham was still working on the lab analysis report and was hoping to have an answer by the next day at the latest. It was that time in a case where everything seems to be dropping in place like a jigsaw puzzle. One piece at a time until it starts to reveal the full picture. The problem with police work is you never have the full picture in the beginning to help you put the puzzle together. You are working in the dark. With everything coming together it is strange how things become calmer and quiet. At this stage of an investigation there is not much that can be done without tripping over your own feet, so JD was reviewing the files of the last body found.

He was reviewing his notes taken with Neal Stephens on the night of the discovery of Claire Shannon and cross referencing them with the formal interview. Something kept niggling him in the back of his mind like he had missed something. JD could not place what was wrong but he had a strong feeling something did not match. That was when the phone rang from the new NCA office.

The National Crime Agency is going to be the new name for the Serious Crime Unit. Some people have started calling it the FBI for the UK. All JD knows is that there are far too many initials out there already without bringing new ones in to remember. The NCA is working alongside the SCU until later in the year when it will go 'live' properly. The phone call from their communications centre gave JD confidence that the new agency may be able to bring something new to the police that has been missing in the past. Cross agency co-operation.

A phone call had been received at the offices of MI6 stating a package was waiting for Claire Shannon at her last known location and DCI Carter should be informed. Why MI6? JD had no idea, but luckily the woman who took the call had recognised Carter's name from the press conference and called the NCA co-ordination room straight away. The fact that Claire Shannon's name had not been released raised a red flag on the NCA computer system and calls were made to the various offices dealing with the case. Within fifteen minutes of receiving the call JD was in a car and on his way to the scene. The two squad cars which beat him to the alleyway were diverted from patrols nearby to set up the road blocks and secure the scene. The road blocks are going to cause hell with the London roads but JD doesn't care.

As he gets out his car an armoured white truck is allowed through the police tape barrier. It has RLC Explosives Ordinance Disposal written in black lettering on the side. Who the hell called the bomb squad? JD thinks.

He walks to the nearest uniformed officer, a tall young man with a shock of blonde hair under his hat and a prominent Adam's apple that bobs up and down as he swallows.

'What's happening son? Have you secured the area and managed to get eyes on the package?'

The constable, already nervous, doesn't know whether to nod or shake his head in answer to the questions. He does a sort of half nod, half shake and ends up circling his head whilst his Adam's apple rapidly shoots up and down. JD tries not to notice.

'Sir, we secured the area but we haven't gone into the alleyway.'

A bob of the Adam's apple.

'We did not receive clearance to do that and we thought we had best leave for the detective in charge. You, sir.'

He looks around at the EOD van.

'Is it a bomb sir? Another terrorist attack like 7/7?'

JD places his left hand on the young man's arm, he can't reach the shoulder.

'It's OK son. Securing the area was the priority and no we don't think it is a bomb. I don't know who called them out so don't worry about that. Now I need you and your partners over there to start canvassing for witnesses. We need to find out if anybody has been coming in or out of this alleyway or acting suspiciously in the last few hours. Jog on now lad and get back to me with your findings.'

The young man turns to call over the other three officers.

'Son. No shouting. Keep things calm and we all stay calm. Take a walk to them, clear your head and explain to them what I've said to you. Good job on getting here so quick and securing the scene, you can tell them that as well. How long have you been on the force?'

JD consciously ignores his Adam's apple.

'Two weeks, sir. This is my first ride out, it's my familiarisation today.'

'Well you've done well. We'll make a copper of you yet.'

Relief floods the young constable's body and JD notices he stands slightly taller.

'Thank you sir, I'll get back to you with any findings.'

He turns and walks away. JD feels a smile coming but stops it when he remembers why he is here. He starts to make his way to the alleyway.

'Stop that man!'

The shout makes JD turn around expecting trouble. His body is tensed waiting for a physical attack that doesn't come.

'You! What in the bloody hell do you think you are doing?'

The soft lilting Welsh valley accent seems out of place coming from the huge man mountain bearing down on JD.

'No bugger enters that area until I clear it. Who are you?'

JD holds out his hand.

'Acting DCI Dawkins of the Metropolitan police and head of this investigation and this is my crime scene. Now who the fuck are you?'

A huge smile reveals two missing front teeth in the face of the man now only a few feet away. He stretches out his hand, 'Pleased to meet you DCI Dawkins, Sergeant Gerwin Horleston of the EOD at your service, and until I clear it this is my fucking crime scene.'

JD cannot help but smile along with the man now gripping his hand with a force strong enough to crush rocks. They size each other up, both grinning like loons. JD breaks first.

'Let's talk Sergeant. It looks like we both want the same thing.'

They break their grip.

'Now who called you out?' JD asks.

'Well, it's like this, we are now all on the NCA call out list. I would imagine we have the Fire, Ambulance and the bloody Wombles on the way too. All we've been told is that a suspicious package has been left at this location and I am not going to let anyone near it until I make sure it's safe.'

JD looks him up and down.

'They put you in one of those bomb suits? I don't mean to be offensive, but you're a big old unit.'

JD receives a slap on the back that would knock a normal sized man over. Gerwin is laughing out loud.

'Don't be fucking silly, can you see me getting down on my hands and knees with my face on the floor. No mate, I've got Johnny 5 over there to do the dirty work.'

He points over his shoulder and JD sees two men in camouflage fatigue putting ramps into place at the back of their van and guiding a tracked robot out using a remote control.

'Now then Mr Dawkins, shall I clear your crime scene for you?'

CHAPTER 22

Graham is astounded by the amount of violent crime that takes place in London. When he was head of forensic sciences in Leeds he would see maybe ten violent murders in a year. In the two years he has been with the Metropolitan forensics unit he has dealt with that number a month at some times. At least this one isn't related to the Ripper inquiry, he thinks to himself. He looks at the scene before him and starts to theorise the way in which this poor soul managed to end up dead at the back of a closed down DIY store car park with his throat cut. He speaks into a small digital voice recorder.
'Deceased is a male, white in his mid 30's. Found by a member of the public approximately one hour ago, air temperature 6 degrees centigrade, external body temperature 91.2 Fahrenheit. Approximate time of death from body temperature drop would be between four and five hours ago. Around ten hundred hours this morning.'
He continues surveying the murder scene carefully as his forensics team take photographs of the body and the general area from all angles.
'You finished here David.' He says to the photographer nearest the body. The hooded figure nods his head.
'Thanks.'
He leans down and carefully feels around the face and jaw. 'Both corneas are clouded and rigor mortis has begun. There is stiffening to the facial muscles and jaw,' he moves his hands down the neck, avoiding the gaping wound, and on to the shoulders and upper arms, 'no muscular stiffening to the upper torso, but the ambient temperature will be slowing the process down somewhat I imagine.'
He examines the wound more closely.

'Fatal wound to the throat by a bladed instrument causing massive blood loss. The body is bare from the waist up and no other injuries are apparent to the torso. The primary examination shows just one wound, the fatal one to the throat.'

He once again notes the lack of blood around the body. 'Victim has been moved post mortem to this location. This is suspected due to no indications of blood loss in the area around the body.'

Opening the small metal case he has with him Graham removes a scalpel and a thermometer. Using the sharp blade he makes a nick about half a centimetre long in the rib margin on the right hand side of the body. He pushes the thermometer into this gap until he feels the resistance he knows to be the liver. Steadying the body with one hand he sharply stabs the thermometer forward and feels it pierce the liver.

'Due to the single wound the body core temperature is recorded by measuring liver temperature. Rectal temperature recording not attempted.'

A body temperature is normally around 98.6 Fahrenheit and drops by 1.5 degrees every hour until it reaches the ambient temperature. The problem with using only this method to determine time of death is that it can be affected by air temperature, moisture and other climatic factors. Taking a core body temperature is much more accurate. Other Drs may have used a rectal temperature reading but with there being no other injuries to the torso, Graham knows that the liver temperature will reveal time of death more accurately.

'Core body temperature 92.3 Fahrenheit, estimated TOD confirmed.'

Removing the thermometer from the liver he places it into a small plastic, zip-lock bag and puts it back into the case. He seals the small incision with simple sticking tape and stands up. He will be completing a more thorough examination of the body at the morgue.

Ensuring he has left no conflicting evidence at the scene he makes his way back to the Scene of Crime Officer.
'Well, that's me done here. Provisional findings are that the time of death was around 10am this morning from a single stab wound to the throat. The body has been moved to this location after death as can be seen by the lack of blood in the area. I will do a more detailed examination on him later when he gets to the labs. No identification found with the body so we have e-mailed a photo back to the unit and my guys are running facial recognition. Oh… and we have the dental forensics team back at the offices who will also try to identify the victim. That's it from me as far as the crime scene goes.'
The SOCO nods and thanks Graham for his time and expertise.
Leaving his team to finish up around the crime scene, Graham removes his coveralls, boots and gloves. He places his tools into the back of his Skoda Octavia estate, gets into the driving seat and takes a deep breath. Whilst he is working he sees the body as just another piece of evidence to work on but when he stops he recognises that another human life has been taken in a violent manner. He wipes a shaky hand across his mouth and starts the car. 'I Giorni' by Ludovico Einaudi emanates from the CD player. The soft piano melody soothes Graham as he makes his way back through the London traffic to his offices. His offices for the dead.

CHAPTER 23

'What does he want us to do with these?'
Zoe is holding the objects that have just been thrown into the room and examining them. Small bits of sharp metal attached to a short Velcro strap.
'They look like mini knives, what are they? Helen? What are they for?'
Helen picks up four of the small items and starts to place them on the fingers of her right hand. The curved metal parts lie underneath the fingers between first and second knuckles.
'Now he wants us to fight. It will only last a few minutes and you must not attack the head. He will kill you if you mark the face, then he will kill me. Put on the blades then put on the mask. He will be back in a moment. When it is over he will fuck one of us, I will try and make sure it is me…I am used to it now.'
Zoe starts sobbing quietly as she attaches the Velcro to her fingers.
'I…I am not sure I can do this Helen.'
'You can, you must and you will. He seems to know which girls are fighters. When he picked you up he must have seen something in you that he knew would make you fight. He's made one mistake in his choice of girls and she's in the corner waiting to be taken apart.'
Zoe thinks back to her argument with Richard in the bar. She must have been watched that night and that is the reason she is here, her aggression towards Richard is the cause.
'Oh God.' Is all Zoe can say.

'Zoe, make sure your mask is on before he comes in. These are different to the last, we can see in these. He wants us to see each other when we fight. Don't worry about hurting me, I am going to be doing the same to you, but try and use your left hand when hitting most of the time. That way less damage is done but you will need to use the blades. You must cut me and I must cut you. Do you understand?'
There is no response,
'Zoe! Do you understand what we have do?'
Quietly, 'Yes, I understand.'
A minute after they have both put on their leather hoods the door opens.
'Showtime ladies, let's make it a good one today. I want blood and I want lots of it. If I don't get that I will cut it myself from your bodies. Let's go.'
For a moment Helen is tempted to attack the large man who is in the doorway issuing instructions. She only stops herself when she remembers the treatment doled out to the girl who tried to escape. She does not want to hear those anguished screams coming from her own mouth. She is a fighter, she will survive.
She turns to Zoe, 'I'm sorry.', and walks through the door past their tormentor.
Zoe follows meekly.

'We've got a feed!'
Luke realises he has just shouted out to an empty room. His work on the encrypted live stream over the last few hours appears to have paid dividends. He starts to work on identifying the source as he picks up the phone and dials JD's number. Getting no answer he hits the Superintendent's speed dial button.

'Ma'am, I can't get hold of DI Dawkins but I have cracked the live stream from our suspect…No, no location as yet but I'm working on that. I am also recording the feed and analysing the links that are jumping on to the feed. There are a lot of them and more coming in. These are easier to locate, not all are using encryption or it's encryption that we know the source code for.'

Luke nods into the phone, 'Yes ma'am, in the IT lab. If you are coming down any chance of a coffee?'

Luke knows he is pushing his luck but he enjoys pushing people's buttons to see how they react. 'Thank you ma'am, much appreciated. I take it Julie Andrews.'

He waits for the question but Superintendent Wilks has been around a while, she knows he is baiting her. Luke gives in, 'You know ma'am, Coffee, white, none.'

He allows himself a cheeky grin as the phone gives out its disconnected tone in his ear.

'Gotcha!', and he's not just talking about the video feed this time.

He tries again to call JD but his mobile goes straight into voice-mail.

'Where are you JD?' Luke voices out loud before leaving a message.

JD at that moment is looking over the EOD expert's shoulder and looking at a small colour screen.

'Tell me why we can't have our phones and radios on again.' Gerwin sighs, he gets fed up of saying the same thing at each incident. Surely the Met run seminars and training on this sort of thing, he thinks.

'Right. We don't know what is in that package,' he points to the box that is in the middle of the screen in front of him, 'if it is a radio controlled device, or uses a mobile signal then your phone or radio, when it transmits, could set it off. It's a slim possibility but we don't want to take that risk. Your phone, even if it is not making a call, automatically sends out tracking signals to the nearest cell phone masts to ensure it is using the strongest signal. That has been known in the past to be enough to cause a connection to the device, albeit in the labs.'

'OK, I understand. Now what's the plan of action with that box, we can't have it blown up, we need to see what's inside.'

Gerwin points to a small graph on the side of the screen.

'It looks like we may be in luck. See this? This shows us what Johnny 5 over there is sniffing out using amplified fluorescence polymers to detect minute particles of explosive traces. We are not seeing anything above normal here.'

He moves the joystick on the control panel attached to the small, rugged screen. The picture moves slightly and a robotic arm extends out towards the box.

'If there's a trip switch, this where you might want to cover your ears.'

He looks over to his colleagues and nods his head. They each pull out folding ear defenders and place them on their heads.

'Health and safety mate, bloody health and safety. I can't be arsed with it myself.'

The pincers on the end of the metal arm slowly open. When they are wider than the width of the box the arm extends further. With a slow fluid movement Gerwin closes the pincers around the box and reverses the remote vehicle out carefully. There is no explosion.

JD realises he has been holding his breath and lets out a large 'whoooof' of air.

After moving backward a metre the robot is stopped and the pincers retract slightly.

'Shall we take the money or see what's in the box?', Gerwin smiles and turns to JD, 'It's your choice but the crowd are chanting for the box.'

He waves a finger in the air in a circular motion and his crew take their ear defenders off. One comes running over carrying a helmet with a full face clear visor.

Taking the helmet from the young man, Gerwin gives him the remote and screen and places the helmet on his head.

'Time for a fat man to get down on his hands and knees and see if God wants him for a moonbeam. Best you stay here.'

As he walks towards the alley way he pulls on a pair of thin, green aviator gloves. The material is thick enough to offer protection from abrasion on the ground, but thin enough to allow for a certain amount of touch and feel. If it was a defusing situation he was getting into, Gerwin would not be wearing gloves at all. No matter how heavy the gloves may be they are not going to stop your hands being blown off as you hold an explosive device within them.

When he reaches the robot JD watches him get down on his hands and knees and then lay flat near the box.

With his outstretched hands he feels around the box for any switch or wires and finds none. Putting his fingertips to the front of the box he slowly inches it open and looks inside. He closes it back up.

JD sees him stand up with the box clutched in his hands and walk towards him. In preparation JD puts on a pair of thin rubber gloves.

'I think this is for you.' Gerwin says as he hands the box over. 'You might not want to open it here,' he nods towards the growing presence of TV camera lights and press photographers, 'it contains a human hand.'

CHAPTER 24

I take Julia to see her father before we head off to the airport to pick up her mother and uncles. There has been no change in his condition, which the Drs say is a good sign, and I see Julia take some comfort from that. From bitter experience I know that injuries like these can take a man's life suddenly even when everything is looking positive. Internal injuries, blood pooling around organs, swelling and infections can all cause a cruel turn to a hopeful situation, but I stay quiet about my misgivings with Julia. I do not wish to upset my new fiancée. We stay with Nektarios for an hour and I watch as Julia holds his hand and tells him about our engagement, tells him she wants to be walked down the aisle by her father. Tells him she loves him and needs for him to come back to her. I feel the prick of tears in my eyes as she does this and realise just how much this woman and her family have come to mean to me in such a short space of time. I place my hand on her shoulder and bend down to whisper softly in her ear,
'We must go. Your family arrives soon and we will come straight back from the airport so you can all be together with your father. Come on Julia, he's going to be all right.'
I take her from the hospital, my arm wrapped around her as she struggles with her emotions. Before we get in to the car I hold her tightly in my arms and kiss her on the forehead, the nose, the lips. I tell her again that everything will be alright while looking into her red-rimmed, puffy eyes. She nods and buries her face into my chest. We stay that way for a few moments while other people making their way through the hospital car park, sensing loss and tragedy, avoid looking at us.

Waiting at the arrivals area of Gatwick airport, of any airport, is something I love. There is always so much emotion from relatives, friends, loved ones, and I feel it gives me hope when I normally only see so much sadness and pain. The young boy running up to his father with a huge grin on his face as he shouts 'Daddeeeeee!' is a joy to anyone who sees it. You cannot help but smile at the raw emotion being shown so unashamedly. The two lovers who have been kept apart for what seems to them an eternity but in reality is probably only a few days, embrace and tell each other how much they missed the other person. Their kisses long and passionate in front of hundreds of strangers who either watch with compassion or cynicism in accordance with the state of their own relationship. The elderly relative who wheels a trolley piled high with suitcases and bags is swarmed over by family members like a queen bee in the hive. Hugs, kisses and assistance coming at every angle until they are overwhelmed by kindness and the tears start to flow.

But then there is the sadness of a journey made from necessity. A death in the family, an illness, or in Julia's case, a serious injury to a close family member. Anna, Stelios and Babis Manousakis walk through the doors, the two men have their heads held high in the Cretan way. Proud, defiant, alert. Anna has aged ten years in the week since I last her at the restaurant. She is dressed head to toe in black as if she is already in mourning for her husband. The two men wear outfits so similar they could be uniforms. Black shoes, blue jeans, a black shirt with two buttons undone at the neck and both carry a leather jacket. The only difference between the two is that Stelios, the younger of the brothers, carries a messenger style bag over one shoulder. I stand back as Julia greets them all. A hug for her mother and a kiss on both cheeks from her uncles. They stand talking together for a minute or two, nods and shakes of heads as questions are asked and answered. Julia says something and they all turn to look at me. I have not felt such scrutiny even when standing in the dock giving evidence at a murder trial. Julia smiles at me through watery eyes and beckons me over. I take a deep breath and walk over to meet my new family.

Back at the hospital I wait outside the High Dependency Unit whilst Julia and her family see Nektarios. I am just trying to make my way through a terrible cup of vending machine coffee when my phone rings and vibrates in my pocket. I check the caller ID, Superintendent Wilks.
'Evening ma'am. Any news on the case?'
'Peter, we have news on the Ripper I need to speak to you personally about. I will not discuss it over the phone but I need to see you urgently. Where are you?'
'At the hospital with Julia's family. I was going to take them back but I can get them to call a cab and come in straight away.'
Peter hears another voice in the background before the Superintendent speaks again,

'Yes, good idea. Peter I will send a blue light round to take them home, we need to see you. Give Julia and her family my best wishes and apologies for the late hour in dragging you away and get here quickly.'

I cannot even say 'Yes ma'am' before she hangs up.

'What the hell is going on?' I say out loud as I bin my crap cup of coffee. My thoughts are tumbling over each other, Helen, the Ripper, missing girls, murder…I walk quickly to the hospital room and pull Julia to one side.

'I think there's been some kind of breakthrough in the Ripper case. Wilks has just called me in to her office ASAP. There will be a police car arriving soon with instructions to take you back home when you need it. I'm sorry but I have to go. I think there may be information about Helen, Wilks said it was personal.'

I kiss her and say 'I love you,' before walking away in a daze, trying not to think of worst case scenarios in my over-imaginative mind…and failing.

CHAPTER 25

The Superintendent's office is crowded. As well as Wilks and the Commissioner there is JD, Graham and Luke, from the IT Forensics department, all crammed in. Only the Commissioner is seated.

'Glad you managed to get here so quickly.' He says almost sarcastically. 'Superintendent Wilks persuaded me to change my mind about having you present for this.'

He swivels in his chair, 'Pat, it's all yours. Let's get this over with.'

She glowers at the back of the Commissioner's head before talking to me.

'Peter, we have information that your sister appears to be caught up in this whole terrible mess. You already know about the teeth marks that were made post mortem to our latest victim being identified but we managed today to hack into an encrypted video stream that you may want to see. Please take a seat.'

She gestures to an empty chair in front of the large plasma screen that dominates the one side of her office. JD places his hand on my shoulder as I sit down and bends to whisper in my ear,

'I wanted to show you this privately but the Commissioner wants to see your reaction. It was his idea to have you here, not Wilks.'

I turn and see the Commissioner watching me intently from his comfortable chair, the Superintendent's chair, behind the heavy desk. He continues looking at me as he talks to JD, 'DI Dawkins, would you get the lights please.'

I feel rather than see JD's heavy footfalls as he makes his way to the light switch. As the overhead lights are turned off, Luke taps away on a wireless keyboard and an image of the Metropolitan Police logo appears on screen. The Superintendent continues her monologue. I haven't said a word since I was ushered in.

'Peter, this was streamed live through the internet at 1830 hours this evening. It was broadcast through an encrypted server and network system to subscribers throughout the world. Luke here broke the encryption and managed to record the events you are about to see. Play the video.'

The screen flickers and shows a brightly lit square of darkly stained concrete. There is a crude form of boxing ring set up using thick ropes wrapped around sharp metal stakes that are embedded into the floor. The room looks large but the lights are concentrated on the ring, the background is an impenetrable gloom.

A man in a black leather or rubber gimp mask enters the ring. He is naked apart from a pair of leather chaps that cover his legs leaving his groin and buttocks exposed. He holds apart the two ropes that form the perimeter and allows two women to enter. The women are also hooded but are completely naked otherwise. The body language of the two women is in complete contrast to each other. The taller woman has her head held high, proud and challenging, the other slightly shorter woman has her head bowed and you can see her body shaking. I can hear sobbing in the background and realise it must be coming from the cowed woman. The man pulls her roughly to him and says something, imperceptible to the microphone, into her ear. At the same time he grabs her right breast savagely and kneads it. Her head jerks upright but the shaking of her shoulders as she sobs continues.

He lowers his head to her other breast and I watch disgusted as he licks and nibbles around the nipple, all the while kneading painfully into the other. He releases her and turns back to the camera his tongue flapping obscenely in and out of the mask.

An electronically altered voice over a heavy rock soundtrack comes from the speakers.

'You wanted girls. You wanted blood. You wanted sex and violence and rock and roll, well tonight your wishes have come true. Our girls are going to fight, bleed and fuck for you like you have never seen before. We will have five rounds tonight, more than normal I know. Why? I hear you cry. Well, tonight we have a new girl. She came to us begging to be put in the ring for your pleasure. But now she is here she has had second thoughts, so we put her here anyway and added two extra rounds to make her think again about fucking us about. We have only had to persuade her once to stay. We need your money to make her return.'

The man in the ring starts rubbing his groin, stiffening as he does so.

'You know what you want, so tell us. You have one minute to get your votes in, no votes no show. It's up to you to decide what you want to see first…make your choice now.'

On screen a list appears in bright red,

ROUND 1
- OPTIONS -

1. Fight then Fuck (Girl Girl) – 50 Credits
2. Fuck then Fight (Girl Girl) – 50 Credits
3. Fight only (Girl Girl) – 40 Credits
4. Fuck Only (Girl Girl) – 35 Credits
5. Fight then Fuck (Girl Boy) – 60 Credits

6. Fuck then Fight (Girl Boy) – 60 Credits
7. Fight Only   (Girl Boy) – 40 Credits
8. Fuck Only   (Girl Boy) – 40 Credits
9. Fight and Fuck   (Girl Girl Boy) – 100 Credits

Behind the list of options the man has turned his attention to the other woman, rubbing his crotch against her whilst spreading her legs with his hands. He rubs her and brings his fingers to his face to lick them. The woman doesn't move a muscle, just lets herself be abused.
JD starts talking,
'At this point there was a huge surge in network traffic to the site. We estimate around 5,000 subscribers voted and paid for an option. Each credit is worth two bitcoins which is equivalent to two US dollars. Even if they all paid for the cheapest option that is $350,000. And they didn't all go for the cheapest option.'
Onscreen option 3 starts flashing as the list around it disappears.
The man grabs the two women and pulls them to him. He seems to be giving orders to them both. The sobbing woman is getting the breast treatment from him again and squirming to try and get away. She stops moving as his head turns to her with more orders, and she nods.
'One minute rounds, maximum pain, maximum pleasure. Lets fight!'
The electronic voice stops, the man walks out of the ring and a clock appears in the top left hand corner. A buzzer sounds and the taller woman lashes out with her left hand slapping cruelly against the others right breast. The shorter woman backs away, her arms going up defensively across her chest. She is followed across the ring and grabbed, their heads come together as they wrestle and I am sure the taller woman is giving orders to the other.

The right hand snakes out from the short woman and rakes across the others buttocks. Streaks of blood shoot across the area where she touched and I recognise the same mark from other victims bodies. I turn my head to Graham quickly and he nods slowly in my direction, I can almost hear his voice in my head, 'I know, I'm sorry.'
The fight goes on for what seems like forever, the minute drags on and on. I realise they have some form of weapon in their right hands and both are managing to use it sparingly. When the buzzer sounds again both women have blood oozing from many small cuts around their body.
'Stop the tape Luke.' Wilks says.
'There are two more rounds of just fighting like this Peter with a ten minute gap between each. The girls are cleaned off between each fight by the man you have seen in the ring and the fourth round involves the two women forced to perform with each other, no fighting. The final round is a different option again. The bastards choose the last option, a fight between all three.'
Luke interjects, 'Ma'am. I'm not sure people are actually deciding the outcome of the options. The algorithms are all wrong for the outcomes. The first two rounds I would say were fight only, but then the numbers changed. I believe that the people behind this are showing what they want while taking the money for other votes.'
The look Wilks gives the young man is withering.
'What in God's name does that have to do with anything. We have sick bastards watching this crap for pleasure and paying money to do it. We have two women suffering who we believe are next on the list as victims of the Ripper and you are worried about damn algorithms that show people are not getting their right fix of this vile sideshow.'
The Commissioner leans forward.

'Hold on Pat. He may be onto something here. If we can inform these… 'he makes a little rabbit ears quotation mark, '…these "customers" that their money is not going where it should we may be able to piss them off enough to complain. If they complain they have to know who to complain to. If they know who to complain to we can track that I presume?' He looks to Luke for acknowledgement and gets a quick nod of the head.
'And if we can track them we can get them. Good work son.' He sits back in the chair. I never figured the old guy for a computer whizz. Once again I am surprised. I feel it is now my turn to speak.
'This is all well and good, but why have I been dragged into this. Ma'am you said it was personal, are you telling me that Helen is one of the women in this video. I can see certain similarities with the taller woman, but even I can't be sure if you are asking for a positive ID.'
Grim faced she turns to Luke.
'Go to the end of the final round. Show him why he is here.' I want to say I don't want to see it. I want to tell them to stop. I have never been more scared in my life than I am now I realise. The iced hand of fear wriggles it way along my spine as Luke starts the video again.

The first thing I notice is that the countdown clock has disappeared. It is the first thing because I do not want to see what is happening on the screen now my fears are almost confirmed it is Helen there. I drag my eyes down towards the unfolding horror.

Both women are grappling on the floor. You can see the exhaustion in their bodies as they try to throw themselves at each other. The stains on the floor I see now, are caused by the blood of the combatants from previous bouts. Both of them are covered in small cuts and the capillary bleeding is mixing with sweat to make their skin slippery and greasy. They keep wriggling out of each others grasp. The man stands behind them. He is wearing a cod piece now. Every so often he pulls them apart and lays in to them with his fists, punching legs and buttocks in the fleshy areas. Maximum pain, minimum damage.

Finally the girls lay spent, exhausted and bloody on the floor. Feeble slaps are directed at each other with hardly any force behind them. No matter what the man does he cannot get them to fight any more. He rips off his codpiece and throws it to one side. Bending down to the small of the two women he pulls her around to a seated position with her back against one of the iron posts and spreads her legs for the camera. He uses his hands on her for a moment before taking a step backwards. He then moves towards the taller girl.

My eyes are already prickling with anger and tears as he drags her over to the other girl and forces her onto all fours in a kneeling position. He places himself behind her and starts thrusting brutally into her. He slows himself and readjusts his position. I see the woman's back arch as he takes her painfully in this new manner, slowly at first and then he builds up the pace. He reaches over and grabs her right hand. He grabs her right hand and forces it to the groin of the smaller woman, rubbing it roughly. Her shrieks are horrifying but what pierces me the most is the one single word that was screamed. One word that preceded the sounds coming from this poor girls body.

The one word was.

'HELEN!'

I cannot move. I am aware of the screen freezing with a picture of my sister being violated and the torture being enforced on the other girl. JD moves forward and turns it off, Graham rushes towards me as he sees me start to slump in the chair. Wilks is angrily glaring at the Commissioner who in turn is watching me with interest. My fists clench and unclench and JD places himself in front of me making eye contact.
'Breathe Peter. Just breathe. Look at me mate, that's it. Keep focussed on me. Deep breaths.'
I cannot think of anything else to say,
'I need a drink.'
JD keeps eye contact,
'We all could do mate. We all could do.'

CHAPTER 26

Helen is exhausted. She is lying motionless on the hard, cold concrete floor. The only movement comes from the rise and fall of her chest as she breathes. Even this small movement is enough to open the network of small cuts across her body to force blood from her wounds. She wants to turn to Zoe and check she is all right, but is too tired to move even her head. When they were dragged back onto the room Zoe had stopped screaming and was releasing only low moans. Those stopped a while ago. Seconds, minutes, hours ago…Helen has no idea as she is drifting in and out of her own dreamlike state within her living nightmare. She notices her hand in front of the face and flexes the fingers tentatively. The ring blades have been removed but her fingers and hand are covered in gore. It looks like she has dipped her hand in red, coagulated paint. She notices the pale skin on her four fingers where the Velcro strapping held the metal in place. She stares at these clean areas, not thinking, not seeing, but just staring at her moving digits as if someone else has control of them.
Her eyes focus on an object beyond her moving fingers. A bowl has been left and next to it is a small bundle of rags. On top of this bundle is a small tube of some kind of cream or ointment and two small bottles of water. Helen's confused mind recognises the bits and pieces gathered on the floor and manages to send a message out through the dimness. 'Clean yourself. Mend yourself. Survive.'
Her brain sends bursts of electricity throughout her body forcing muscles to contract and limbs to move. With gritted teeth Helen pushes herself up on to all fours and drags herself, crawls is the wrong word, over to the objects that have become her mind's centre of attention.

The water is cold to the touch, but refreshes Helen's very soul. She has managed to struggle into a sitting position next to the water bowl and is using a small piece of white cloth to wipe off the blood. Dipping it into the water and slowly moving the damp surface across her skin has a mild revitalising effect on her. She looks towards Zoe and sees how she is slumped in a heap. The raw open skin between her legs is too terrible to contemplate and Helen concentrates on the small pool of blood forming next to Zoe's body. Helen knows the other girl will die if she is not helped and for one brief, awful moment, considers turning away.

She grabs a clean length of cloth and plunges it into the bowl. With one hand she pushes the bowl closer to Zoe and grabs more cloth and the tube of cream. Painfully she moves closer to the younger girl knowing that her own personal survival depends on keeping Zoe alive. Carefully folding a square of cloth she wads it between Zoe's legs to try and stem the bleeding there. A moan escapes from Zoe's lips but nothing else. Helen cleans her fellow prisoners body, wiping the dark blood from her skin and offering words of encouragement as she does so. She is thankful that Zoe does not come round as she completes this task. There will be more than enough pain to come without her having to endure this necessary torture as well.

When it is done, Helen removes the blood soaked cloth from between Zoe's legs. Forcing herself to look at the damage she inflicted she winces at the wounds before her. The bleeding has mostly stopped, the knives are not intended to wound severely, but they do cause a lot of capillary bleeding. Squeezing some cream from the tube Helen gently tries to rub it onto the open cuts to aid healing. Zoe's eye fly open as the stinging cream hits her nerve endings. Screaming out in pain and terror she lashes out with her feet and hands trying to get away, trying to push Helen away.

Helen grabs her and holds her in her arms as the thrashing continues and the screams get louder. She holds her tightly and cries along with Zoe as she offers meaningless words into her ear. Shushing and rocking, holding and stroking she doesn't let go of Zoe until the screaming subsides.
'I'm sorry Zoe. I have to do this. I know it's going to hurt but you have to let me do this. It will sting but it will help. Try not to scream.'
Zoe places her own hand across her mouth to stifle her screams as Helen once more uses the cream to salve the wounds.
'I'm sorry,' said amidst wracking sobs, 'I am so sorry.'
The sounds of the two women continue for many more minutes and carries outside of the room.
The man who sits on an old wooden stool just outside the door, smiles at the sounds. Having showered after the excesses of the previous hour he is refreshed and in a wonderful mood. He is connected to the internet on his Blackberry and is reviewing an e-mail just received.
'Funds Received - $2.2 million. Balance available - $17.63 million. Always a pleasure doing business. Looking forward to the next bout.'
Smiling he types a reply using the small keyboard.
'Excellent few weeks work. It's a shame there is only one more show left. Shall we try somewhere else next year? USA? Vegas?'
Hitting send he is not sure if he will get a response but in a matter of seconds his phone vibrates.
'Sure. Why not!'
His smile is even bigger this time as he pockets the phone and walks away from the locked door, through the old building and finally makes his way outside. As he gets into his car he looks across the river at the city skyline and thinks, 'Why not indeed?'

CHAPTER 27

Graham and JD are both in my office and we are working our way through my bottle of Laphroaig. Wilks left about ten minutes ago to 'have a word with the Commissioner' as she put it. I would love to be a fly on the wall in that room. I cannot help but wonder why the Commissioner wanted me involved in tonight's proceedings. Is he trying to push me in to a corner? Does he want to try and break me? Why…? Question after question running through my mind with no answers.

Graham takes a sip from his glass and closes his eyes in appreciation. He looks at JD,

'Have you told him about the happenings today yet?'

JD shakes his head,

'I was thinking of waiting until tomorrow, but as you brought it up…'

He shifts his muscular bulk in the chair and places his elbows on the table whilst cradling his whisky in his hands. He speaks over the top of the glass,

'We had a phone call today, or more precisely, the NCA received a phone call today via MI6. We were left a gift at the crime scene behind Valascos and the caller wanted to make sure you got it. When I arrived the area was already sealed off and the bomb squad were there, just in case apparently. A small box had been left that contained a human hand. A female hand. We don't know who it belongs to but Graham and his team have been checking it out for evidence.' He turns his gaze to Graham, 'Anything?'

Graham shakes his head.

'Nothing really apart from it appears to have been treated in the same manner as our other victims. It was washed thoroughly after removal from the victim and probably frozen for at least eight hours before being left for us to find.'

I speak up, 'Why freeze the body parts and how do you know a time scale?'

'Well freezing tissue makes it much harder to predict a time of death. Today for example, the body found in the old B&Q car park, I could predict the time of death quite accurately through body temperature, skin lividity, ocular clarity and, though it wasn't required today, insect activity. With a frozen corpse the time of death is confused by the chilling factors on the tissue. When a body is dismembered and bled out it is also a struggle to determine TOD without insect and decomposition activity if it has been frozen. It is lucky we can at least determine an approximate time of freezing of the body due to tissue damage caused by the freeze-thaw process. If the bodies were left in water this would be much more difficult to approximate so at least we have something on our side.'

He takes another sip of his drink. He is on a roll and neither I nor JD wish to interrupt him.

'All of our victims were killed most probably by strangulation. There have been no other identifying kill marks on the bodies. The damage to the oesophagus and neck area due to dismemberment hides most of the distinguishing features of strangulation, but not all. We would normally be able to check for ruptures in blood vessels in the eyes due to their struggling against the strangulation, but we have not found many. I believe the girls have all been unconscious at the moment of death…a small mercy for them. Traces of ACE were found in the toxicology report which would correlate to this assumption.'

I know about ACE. Many TV shows feature a kidnapper using chloroform to knock victims out instantly which is a nice bit of fiction. Chloroform can take anything up to a minute to subdue a struggling person, far too long in the real world. ACE is a mixture of Alcohol, Chloroform and Ether, hence the acronym, and does a far better and quicker job of knocking people out. It also has more chance of keeping your victim alive afterwards. The percentages for accidental death using chloroform alone are not brilliant for your would be kidnapper and violent psychotic torturer.

The irony is not lost on me that I only know about ACE from Helen. In her third year of her Biology and Anatomy degree she had a placement with a research centre near my old place in Battersea. She stayed with me for the month of her placement as it was easier than trying to cross London every morning. One evening she came home feeling nauseous and looking a little excited but vacant, if that makes sense. She couldn't stop talking about an accident in the labs.

Apparently ACE is used on the animals before vivisection by placing a lint cloth soaked with it into a sealed container with the animal. A colleague of Helen's, another degree placement, was transferring a bottle of the liquid from secure storage to the vivisection room when he tripped and fell. He dropped the large bottle containing the mixture which smashed open, spilling around three litres out across the floor. Within seconds people were dropping like flies and it was only the quick thinking of one of the scientists who managed to turn on the extractor fans to full speed that stopped a potential disaster. Helen had been out cold for about ten minutes before being revived. Her colleague, the bottle dropper, was still in hospital under observation. All evening Helen was throwing up and was confused to the point of hilarity. I knew how potent ACE could be. I also knew it wasn't the easiest thing to get hold of.

Graham continues whilst these thoughts are playing in my head.

'It could be assumed of course that our victims have had their throats cut and bled out but I see no evidence of major blood loss prior to death in the major organs. There is no major bruising or damage to the soft tissue around the throat so the strangulation was probably completed by ligature instead of by the killers own hands. A thin cord or wire of some kind. Being unconscious at least it would have been fairly quick on the victims.'

His eyes shift to refocus on the room and not on the victims in his mind.

'It is almost as if at the time of killing he shows compassion on these girls. Like he wants them to have no more suffering.'

'Or he wants to keep them quiet.' JD says flatly.

Graham and I both nod at his statement.

'What about the river water?' I ask

'Inconclusive as the labs suggested. I wish I could say more but all we can definitely say is that it is from the Thames...somewhere.'

'Any news on the e-fit pictures?' I ask JD. Even though I am officially no longer part of the case I want to know everything.

'Nothing apart from the usual sightings from attention seekers. We have uniforms checking out every lead but we all know that for every 500 calls we get, maybe one is useful. We just have to find that needle in the haystack before...'

He stops talking and looks at me. He doesn't need to say the words. He doesn't need to say '...before we find our next victim.'

There is an awkward pause as we are all caught up in our own helpless thoughts. JD masks his own self-consciousness by picking up a file from my desk and flicking through it. I want to change the subject but stay on police issues so I ask Graham about his latest body. The man found in the car park.

'Not a straightforward case Peter. He was moved from the scene of death to the area where he was found. The wound to his throat should have resulted in a huge amount of blood at the scene which was conspicuous in its absence. Even his clothes were virtually bloodless so I believe he was partially dressed before being moved. There is evidence that he recently took part in sexual activity. Traces of semen around the penis and spermicide from a condom were present. My first thought due to the nature of the injury was a rape gone wrong with our victim being the rapist, but why would the rape victim move the body and dress him afterwards? I am not convinced it is a crime of passion either, they are normally more frenzied. More damage to the victim, more stabbings when knives are involved. Perhaps an adulterer, you know, husband walks in, finds a man with his wife and lashes out. But again, that doesn't seem to fit. I can't believe a jealous husband would remove a condom from a dead man who has just been doing the dirty with his wife. The full autopsy is tomorrow morning and I hope it will give us a bit more to work on, if not...'

'Bastard! I knew I had a funny feeling about that guy.' JD stops Graham in mid flow pointing at the report he has been reading.

'Stephens. That homeless guy, this is his army report yes?' I nod, 'Yeah, the desk sergeant gave it to me when we were conducting the interview. Why?'

'The Falklands, Oman, Iraq but that's it. No mention of anywhere else he served.'

'What's your point JD?'

JD puts the file back on the desk in front of him.

'If this is his full report and shows him leaving the army after coming back from Iraq, how come he was not worried about seeing the dismembered body because, and I quote, *'I saw worse in Afghanistan with my unit there'*. Where are the rest of his records and why does it show him leaving the forces? Who is this guy really?'

I cannot believe I missed that glaring piece of information on the day of the interview. Maybe Helen's disappearance has affected me more than I wish to think.
'Let's bring him in if we can find him.'
It is all I can say because I can think of nothing else.

CHAPTER 28

Derek Temple, Commissioner of the Metropolitan Police force, is watching Patricia Wilks pace around his office like a caged jungle beast. All she needs is a long tail swishing angrily from side to side to complete the picture of an angry tiger, he thinks to himself. He knows why she is upset but will not acknowledge the fact that he blamed her for dragging Peter Carter to bear terrible witness to the video a little while earlier on. He sits patiently, waiting for his Superintendent to bare her claws.

She stops and sits down across from him, facing him over his huge desk. Before she voices her opinion, Patricia thinks that if some men use cars as penis extensions then others use office desks for the same job. She looks her superior square in the eye and thinks that here is the biggest penis she has seen in a long time. Taking a deep breath she launches herself at him, 'Sir, I am going to speak freely and I don't give a damn about the consequences. I know your spiel about loyalty and what you think it takes to rise through the ranks but today you showed no loyalty whatsoever to a fellow officer. Today you were a fucking disgrace to the uniform and the position you hold within the Metropolitan force. You not only disgraced yourself but you brought me down with you and that is something I cannot tolerate.'

She takes another breath, half way between a sigh and an intake of air through rage,

'The manner in which you have conducted yourself against a member of my team,' she catches his look, 'Yes Sir!...MY team, is unacceptable. You appear to have a personal vendetta for DCI Carter, first taking him off the case after embarrassing him in a public interview and now this. Just what are you trying to do to the man? What are you trying to do to this case? You have personally sabotaged one of the best detectives we have and caused untold damage and delay to the investigation.'

Derek Temple sits back in his chair, his manner relaxed. This only serves to enrage Wilks further but she knows better than to respond. She bites her lip and looks out over the cityscape knowing if she continues she will be handing her uniform and warrant card in to the reception area on her way out.

'Patricia. Pat. There are things going on here that I am not at liberty to discuss. When...If, you ever reach this,' he sweeps his hand around the office, 'level of advancement in your career you will understand that. For now I will forgive this outburst as a sign of irritation over how the investigation is going. I will not take it personally, I know that women sometimes have outbursts they cannot control...'

'What! Did you really just say that? You fu..'

'Patricia...stop and think before you go on with your words in my office. I will only tolerate so much. Even from you.'

Wilks stands up her fists clenched and pushed into the desk before her.

'And they say institutionalised sexism and racism has been eradicated from the Met. Oh what absolute bollocks that is.' She jabs her finger angrily at him, 'You are not worthy to even wear the uniform of the Met, let alone be its Commissioner. I wonder what the IPCC will do when they hear what I have to say about your behaviour.' She counts off on her fingers, 'One, deliberate interference with an ongoing investigation. Two, undermining an officer's authority in front of the public. Three, jeopardising the well-being of an officer.

Four, blaming another officer for your misappropriate actions.

Five, oh and this is the one I love the most, overt sexist comments to a fellow officer. I hope they kick you out instead of forcing a resignation by early retirement.'

As she turns to storm out of the office Derek makes her pause, 'Give my regards to Dan Millward, the head of the IPCC won't you. If you are going straight there now, please let him know I'll pick him up for golf at 9 a.m. tomorrow, there's a good girl. Of course if you decide to not bother telling tales to the nearest school yard prefect, we will continue this discussion in the morning when you have calmed down and are not so, shall we say, tired and emotional. Be here for 0700 hours if you choose the second option. Don't be late, I have an urgent appointment at nine.'

Wilks' face is bright red as she leaves the office. The young constable who is walking towards her in the corridor instantly dives out of her way as he sees the look on her face. Wilks didn't even notice him so intense is her anger.

CHAPTER 29

'JD, get on to the Army records office. See what they can give us. It was all a bit coincidental that his records were waiting at the desk just when we needed them. I'm not sure what's going on here but it's enough to get me interested in this Stephens character all over again.'

JD grunts, 'It's the MOD we're talking about here. We will have to wait for office hours. They can't fight a war outside of 9 to 5 Monday to Friday.'

I think back to the interview.

'What happened with his prints and DNA sample?'

Graham joins the conversation, 'All clean. Nothing at all from them.'

'All clean?' I look at JD and see a quizzical look mirrored back at me, 'But he was arrested the week before for an assault, his prints should be on file.'

JD nods his agreement as he grabs the phone off my desk. 'On it.' He says.

We have now all put our whisky tumblers on the table and turned to more interesting matters. I check my watch, 21:40 and pull out my mobile phone.

'Who are you calling?' Graham asks.

'My brother Paul. If anyone knows how a man can seemingly drop out of the army yet end up in Afghanistan, he will.'

I know it's late in Greece, they are two hours ahead of UK time, but I also know that they stay up later over there. The locals think nothing of going out for an evening meal at 11pm at night. I just hope Paul has turned local. If not he is about to get a rude awakening.

His assured voice answers the phone after two rings.

'Hey little brother, what's up at this time of night?'

In the background I hear chatter and the clink of metalware on plates. Good, I think, he has gone native.

'Paul, I need some information. Can you talk somewhere a bit privately.'
I can almost see him nodding at the other end. I hear him speak to someone,
'Just a minute guys, it's my brother. Carry on without me, I have to take this.'
The sound of diners and people enjoying their evening increases as he moves through the taverna and then I hear a door opening and close. Instantly the background noise stops.
'Go ahead Peter, what can I do for you?'
I close my eyes.
'If a soldier leaves the army and rejoins what happens to his records? Do they stop and restart or would there be two separate records for him? I mean, if a guy leaves in 2004 and rejoins in say 2005, would there be two independent personnel records for him?'
There is a pause as Paul considers my request.
'From what I recall the records are re-opened when the individual rejoins. It happens more often than you think so there are quite a few cases of records with blank periods. Of course the other reason would be if the guy has gone to the Jedis or the Walts.'
I shake my head,
'What are you on about mate? Jedis? Walts?'
A laugh down the phone,
'Sorry Pete, SF or Int. You know Special Forces, the SAS, SBS or he's gone green slime on you and gone to one of the intelligence units like 14 Int cell. Something like that. Then there may be a blank area on the records apart from the phrase 'Under Secondment'. Is that what you are looking at?'
Another shake of my head,
'All we have is a guy's records that show him getting out of the army a few years back, but when we spoke to him he spoke about being in Afghanistan and seeing his mates getting blown up.'

'Have you considered he was on the circuit, sorry...doing specialist contract work, body guarding or convoy work? There are shitloads of guys doing that when they get out.'
'He said he has been on the streets since leaving the army. Doesn't sound like he was doing that sort of thing.'
'Peter, what regiment was he in originally according to the records?'
'RMP, why?'
'Did he leave just after the invasion of Iraq?'
I am now instantly alert.
'How did you know that?'
'Peter, there were a lot of guys who moved across into a very murky area during that time. Working with the Israelis and the Yanks and I have to say there were some strange rumours floating about concerning them. Be very careful here Peter. These guys take no prisoners and do anything to get the job done. They don't believe in collateral damage as being a bad thing. If you're in the way you are a legitimate target and they have very powerful people behind them to back them up. Watch your back little brother, and if you want my advice, forget about this character and move on.'
I mumble my thanks into the phone and tell him to get back to his friends and family. Before I can hang up he says one more thing that stuns me,
'Congratulations on your engagement as well. I know you're busy but I thought you would have let me know earlier than this.' He laughs again, 'You're a lucky man, Julia is a stunner and her family are great.'
'How did you know about that, Christ it was only yesterday morning I asked her.'
'Greek family, mate. Greek family. They can't hear about an occasion like that without throwing a party. Give her my best and tell her we are all pulling for her father. He has many friends over here if he needs any help...and the same goes for you too Peter. You need any help, call me.'
There is a pause from 1700 miles away,

'Have you got an army number for this guy. I know a few people who might be able to help fill in the gaps and I know you wouldn't be asking for help with this if it wasn't a matter of life and death.'

It hits me then that he doesn't know about Helen's disappearance and her involvement in the Ripper investigation. He doesn't watch any UK news in Crete to see the press reports. I don't have it in me to tell him, besides, it's a confidential police matter I lie to myself. Instead I reel off the number in Stephens' file.

'I'll get back to you tomorrow mate. Say hi to Helen when you see her and tell her not to be a stranger. I haven't heard from her in weeks. Take care.'

I hold the phone to my ear a few moments longer than necessary after he hangs up to gather my thoughts.

'Sounds promising,' Graham states, 'what does he say?'

I place the phone on top of the desk.

'We may be looking at special forces or worse case scenario some kind of multi-national black ops operative.'

They both start laughing until they see my face. JD is the first to speak,

'Jesus, you're being serious. What the hell is going on here?'

'That's what we aim to find out and we need to find out ASAP. Is he part of the kidnapping and murders, is he part of a team after the same guy as us, or was he quite simply in the wrong place at the wrong time?'

Graham as always is the voice of reality and pragmatism,

'Or are we simply just barking up the wrong tree and wasting our time?'

JD and I both look at each other. We know that we have depended on hunches in the past to crack cases and we both have the same hunch about this guy. The problem is we have both been known to be wrong as well. My office becomes an area of intense activity as we start calling other departments for information and assistance with our new area of investigation.

We all know that we will not get much sleep again this night.

CHAPTER 30

The grey morning light of dawn filters through into my office. I look around and see how it appears as though a whirlwind has gone through it picking up random items and placing them where it wishes. JD is crashed out in the hard backed armchair in the corner. His jacket is placed over him as a makeshift blanket. I would have thought that he would be a snorer but he lies there as peacefully as new born baby. I gave Graham the cot and he is currently making use of it behind my desk. He is snoring away merrily. That is the reason I cannot sleep and I wonder to myself how JD manages his peaceful slumber through the god awful racket. It has been a tiring night but I am grateful that both men, both friends, stayed here with me to try and gain some answers whilst the rest of the city slept.

JD had the most luck with his enquiries to a small army unit just outside of Hereford. After explaining the situation and performing a face to face video conference with the duty officer there it was agreed that details would be securely e-mailed about Stephens' involvement with what the officer called 'The Det'. A heavily redacted file was sent to us around two hours later.

In early 1999 Stephens had volunteered to join the 14th Intelligence Signals Detachment, *The Det*. Completing his training he was sent to Northern Ireland during the height of the troubled peace process to join the unit in their work against the various terrorist organisations struggling to make their voices, and their bombs, heard in what was a confused time for Northern Ireland. Individual operations were blacked out in the document, along with key dates and individual names, but it appeared he served with distinction until an inquiry was set up over a civilian being killed by the security forces. The young woman who was killed was married to a known IRA sympathiser and was a barmaid in a pub frequented by members of The Det, even though it was officially off limits to the British forces. It seemed the members of the unit were not always ones to follow orders to the letter, yet a blind eye had been turned by their superiors due to the nature and danger of their tasks.

The woman, Noola McCarthy, was killed during a brawl in the pub that turned deadly. Locals had tolerated the English coming into the bar for years. It was a favourite haunt of the construction contractors who were helping to rebuild the city, short and long term contracts meant that there was always a wealth of new faces at the bar. That is why The Det guys fitted in so well and it also gave them a perfect cover story. On the night Noola was killed an argument had broken out over a football game on the television. Rangers versus Celtic is a passionate affair at the best of times but in an Irish pub in a Catholic district it was pure hatred. According to the official report by the security forces a fight had broken out during the game and knives were produced by a number of local men. The Det members in the bar were trying to make their way out when one of them was stabbed in the arm. Stephens defended the injured man relieving the attacker of his weapon and breaking his jaw and right arm in the process. As he bent over to retrieve the knife he was grabbed on the shoulder and instinctively turned around to face what he thought was another attacker. Unfortunately the knife in his hand was plunged into the stomach of Noola McCarthy as she was coming to check he was not injured. The blade was deflected upward by a large metal belt buckle she was wearing and pierced vital organs. She died from massive blood loss at the scene.

This was not the story related by the locals. Their version of events is that Stephens and the man he was with got into an argument over something, the origin of the fight is not known, but it was believed to be over Mrs McCarthy. It was speculated that Stephens and the bar maid had been meeting illicitly for sexual encounters while her husband was away on business. Knowing the husband's business it may have been likely that Stephens was pumping her for information as well as just pumping her. Whatever the reason for the fight, Stephens produced a knife and managed to stab his colleague in the arm before some of the locals rushed in to stop him. This is where one man's jaw and arm were broken. Things now get very confusing, some say he then launched himself across the bar at Mrs McCarthy, others that she came running up to him. All that is known that at this point she received a fatal stab wound to the abdomen. Other members of the security forces were just arriving at this point and can only corroborate the fact that Stephens was found holding the lifeless body of the barmaid.

The two conflicting stories were put down to the troubles of the local Catholic support for the IRA against the security forces. What was interesting was that Stephens was RTU'd, Returned To Unit, immediately following the inquiry. Supposedly for his own protection, but the other man involved stayed in Northern Ireland with The Det.

I wished we could find out the identity of the other man involved to get his version of events but the officer at Hereford informed us he is still a serving member of the forces and until we get an official warrant his identity will remain a secret.

Graham went through the autopsy report and uncovered an astonishing and chilling find. Noola McCarthy's body was covered in small scars as if from a miniature knife. Her and her husband were fond of body scarification was the answer to this conundrum, but we all couldn't help but think back to the video we had watched earlier.

An quick internet search was remarkably enlightening;

Finger knives £12.95

a set of foldable finger knives used mainly for modern scarification. Comfortable to wear and the ability to achieve fine control over the scarification process make these knives an ideal choice for the beginner and professional alike.
By folding the knives a finger interface is created, this is possible due to the flexible quality of the metal and allows for well defined precision.

The images of the items brought up were very similar to those my sister and her opponent were wearing. I am still waiting for a reply from some of the online shops that sell these, but that is a real long shot as there are hundreds of them out there in the UK alone. It seems scarification is more commonplace than I imagined but it just seems too much of a coincidence to see them used on a woman in Stephens' past as well as in use during our kidnap and murder investigation. We are all starting to believe that he is somehow mixed up in this and his homeless situation was just an act.

I yawn as I watch the sun make a feeble attempt at breaking through the cloud before being hidden from view just as quickly as it appeared. Rubbing my hand over my chin I feel the growth of two days of stubble but choose to ignore it as my electric razor would probably wake my two sleeping partners. They need the rest and I am enjoying the calm before they awake from their few hours of sleep.

'I need a coffee.' I say softly to myself and turn towards the door.

JD adjusts his position in the chair and rumbles,

'Wondered when you'd get onto that. Coffee, white, one for me, oh, and see if you can rustle up a sandwich or two. I'm starving.'

I smile at the rumpled form of my partner and a voice pipes up from behind my desk,

'A nice cup of Earl Grey for me and a bacon sarnie wouldn't go amiss.'

At least Graham has stopped snoring.

The small cafeteria is one of the best things the Met has done in my opinion. Open 24 hours, it allows those working at whatever time of the night or day a place to get away from their desks and casebooks and offers them a chance to recharge their batteries. It is never crowded but there are always people milling around, chatting, or just staring deeply into a cup of hot liquid. Luke is doing just that. His head, slightly to one angle rests on one hand. The cup in front of him may once have held hot coffee but there is now a thick film of milk skin that covers the surface. He looks like he too has been up all night. I walk over to his table.
'Hi Luke, can I get you a refill?'
He jerks upright and I realise he was asleep. I curse inwardly for waking him.
'Uh…what…where…Oh, DCI Carter. Morning sir.'
He runs his hands through his hair and down across his face. He has yet to see stubble at this time of the day and I wonder how I must look to him. He suddenly registers the question that woke him.
'Great sir, yes…I mean that would be nice. Coffee Julie Andrews please.'
I smile, 'White nun, I get it.'
He pushes the cold cup away from him as I walk off to get him a fresh cup, JD and Graham can wait for theirs. They need their beauty sleep anyway.

CHAPTER 31

'You did good in the ring girls. Both of you did real good. If you keep that up then no one has to get hurt, at least not seriously.'
He laughs cruelly and throws a package into the room. His silhouette framed in the bright doorway means no features can be seen but he is wearing a mask anyway. The fact he wants to keep his face hidden gives Helen some hope. If he was going to kill them both he would have no reason to hide his features from the two of them.
'Have something to eat. There's a few happy meals in there. You have to keep your strength up and the toys can help you pass the time while I'm gone. He leans outside the doorway allowing bright artificial light to spill into the room. When he turns back he is holding two metal buckets which he places in the centre of the room. One is empty apart from a large serrated knife, the other is full of water.
'I will be back in a few hours. I want the hands from the remaining girls, wash them and keep them submerged in the bucket until I return.'
He walks back towards the door. Helen sees Zoe reaching over for the knife whilst their kidnappers back is turned. The pain as Zoe moves her injured body is evident on her face as she grimaces with each movement. Helen grabs her wrist and shakes her head, mouthing a silent, 'No'. Zoe's defiant look surprises Helen. She thought the fight had been beaten and cut from her during the bout yesterday. She was wrong.
The door closes with a slam and they hear the words, 'Enjoy your meal.' followed by another cruel laugh as the man leaves them once again.
'I could have got him with knife.' Zoe hissed.

'It's not as easy as that. We have to wait for the right time. He is strong and we are no match for him until we can recover, until you can recover. For Gods sake you can hardly move without crying out in pain. He'd snap you like a twig and then come for me.'

'I could have stabbed him and you could have finished him. You're strong, you can do that…'

'Not yet. We have to wait for the right time.'

Zoe's laugh is an angry one, 'But there will never be a right time, will there?'

She may be angry but a little of the fight has left her voice and her body language has altered subtly. She is back to looking like a caged, wounded animal, which is what they both are, Helen thinks.

'Let's eat.' She pulls the paper bag towards them both and hands Zoe one of the brightly covered cardboard boxes from inside. Both of them are salivating at the smells that are emanating through the thin material. Neither one of them wants to think about the command that was given until after they have finished their meal. They take their time and eat slowly, willing the other one to finish first. To finish their meal and pick the knife out from the bucket to complete the terrible task they have been given.

The man outside the room had been expecting an attack from one or both of the girls. The small torch like device attached to his belt was in fact a powerful taser imported from Germany. It would send 50,000 volts of electricity direct to the exposed skin and cause instant paralysis as the nerve endings and brain synapses were assaulted by the electric jolt. He had hoped to use it today but, as he pulls off his hood, he knows it is only a matter of time before he will get the chance and he knows he is going to enjoy his victim's reaction to the weapon. He takes the taser from his belt and places it carefully with the hood on the old wooden desk in the corner of the room. Opening the left hand drawer he pulls out a pair of soft black leather gloves which he puts on and a plain cotton drawstring bag. One of many that is stacked neatly within. He hums a nameless tune as he makes his way through a doorway and into a dark room. He flicks a switch and illuminates a room humming with the sound of refrigeration units and the occasional rattle of a compressor. A large walk-in freezer dominates one wall and he walks purposefully to the heavily insulated door, still humming his tune. He pulls on the long stainless steel handle to open the door and a light flickers on as he steps inside. There are four heavy duty black oxford cotton holdalls on one shelf. He grabs one of the empty bags, zips it open along its length and places it on the floor between his legs. Moving his body slightly to his left he picks out two objects from a low shelf and places them in the bag. He always puts the legs in first. On the shelf above at chest height lies a woman's naked torso. He lifts it carefully off and places it gently into the bag on top of the legs that are already there. Next follows the arms which fit neatly down the side of the bag. He spends a moment staring at the contents of the bag, silent now except for his breathing. Small clouds of his breath appear and disappear in the cold air of the freezer as he stands there slowly tilting his head from side to side to see the handiwork from different angles. He bends forward slightly before standing up, apparently satisfied he has done a good job. He brings his gaze up from the bag and looks straight ahead at the shelf on the far wall. A single human head stares back.

'Time for you to leave babe.'

He picks up the head with a tenderness that was not shown to the woman when she was alive.

'Are you ready to go Valerie?'

He brushes a few strands of hair away from the cold dead face.

'I won't let that witch bite you like she did the last one. She did that just to spite me. She knows you have to be left untouched.'

With each word his face has been getting closer to the white flesh in his hands until he is mere centimetres away. He closes his eyes and takes a deep breath through his nose as if to take in a sweet, heady perfume. With Valerie Ross's severed head in his hands he proceeds to kiss her cold, dead lips with his. When he has finished he gazes lovingly at the face before him.

'Goodnight sweetheart. Thanks for staying with me but it's time for you to go home now.'

He places the head into the cotton bag and pulls the drawstring bag shut.

'God bless.'

Humming his happy tune again he picks up the holdall and makes his way out of the freezer. As he is closing the door a shrill ringing from his mobile phone interrupts his humming. Sighing impatiently he places the holdall on to the ground and reverently puts the cotton bag atop it.

'Yes, what do you want?'

The briefest of pauses.

'That is just what I was about to do, stop fretting and keep your nose out of my business. I am just going to drop one of the girls off…yep…yep..of course…look trust me. None of the girls will talk about who we are or what we do. You have my word on that, they're professionals OK. I'll see you at the club later…yeah…do that. Bye.'

He hangs up the phone and jams it into his coat pocket.

'Fucking muppet.'

He picks up the two bags and makes his way out of the building, stopping only once on his way to the club to drop someone off.

CHAPTER 32

I place the steaming mug of coffee down in front of Luke and he smiles appreciatively.

'Thanks sir. You don't know how much I need this, this morning.'

He wraps his hands around the hot ceramic almost protectively and looks down at the liquid inside. He looks apprehensive.

'You know about the videos don't you sir?'

I sip my coffee and nod, 'I was called in to watch one last night.'

He looks up, 'Your sister?'

'Yes. It was Helen.'

'Oh shit. I'm sorry, I can't imagine what that must have been like for you. At least we have a lead on the others.'

This is news to me.

'What others? Other videos, other girls, or is it more…more of Hel..' I can't say her name again. It won't leave my throat, '…more of my sister?'

Luke's surprise is shown on his face as he looks at me.

'You didn't know? We have managed to trace seven more recorded feeds on secure loops showing the same format, but with different girls in the ring. We have even found a reseller of the videos on the dark web. He has been tracked to a small town called Keighley in Yorkshire. Personally I don't think he is part of this, I think he has managed to get hold of a copy of a fight somehow and is just selling them on to try and make some money from the sickos out there.'

'What makes you think that?'

'He's too sloppy. He has not even attempted to hide his tracks or manipulate his IP address. Anyone with an ounce of common sense would at least use an IP blocker to stop the broadcast of their location. He's even using Paypal and a genuine e-mail address to collect the profit. I reckon it's a teenager in his bedroom doing things his parents have no idea about. It wouldn't surprise me when we knock on his door this morning if he got the original in the school yard from a friend of a friend who knows a guy somewhere. That's a dead end as far I can foresee.'

He takes a tentative sip of the hot coffee.

'What about the other feeds? Do you have any good news about those?'

'Now that's the challenge. I have been in the labs all night tracing, decrypting and generally chasing my tail trying to get a defined location of the source. I have found there are three separate servers broadcasting the feeds on a loop. Again it's a subscription service to log on to but the good news is that one of the servers is based in the US where we have good relations and information sharing is a tried and tested formality. They have already shut it down and raided the building where the server is based.'

He looks at his watch, 'That was about two hours ago. They even streamed the live feed of the operation to us. I watched it and it was like something out of a Tom Clancy novel I tell you. I knew they had some state of the art kit, but it blows our IT department and budget out of the water. What I'd give for some of their hardware.'

He looks across to me , 'Sorry sir, getting sidetracked.'

I motion for him to continue but wonder why JD or myself were not privy to this information.

'Would you like to see it?' he asks.

'After you tell me about the other videos. Have you identified the girls in those yet?'

He pulls a thin, book like object from the delivery style bag that is on the seat next to him. Opening the cover he powers up a tablet PC and start swiping his fingers across the screen and tapping rapidly. He turns the device to face me and I see the screen rotate automatically as he tilts it. The screen is split into three pictures all just about recognisable of the same woman.

'Victim number one, Alison McCormick AKA Indya. The picture on the left is from the missing person file, the centre photo is an enlargement of a still from one of the video feeds and the third is from an arrest mugshot. You can see they are all the same woman.'

He leans over and swipes the screen, another three photos appear.

'Claire Shannon.' He points at the pictures on the screen from above while I watch, 'Missing person report, video still and morgue photo.' He swipes again and a still picture from one of the videos appears.

'Here you can see the two deceased.'

I nod and point to the screen , 'Alison McCormick and Claire…', I move my finger to the other girl who I recognise as Claire Shannon but as I do so the screen moves with the touch of my finger. Valerie Ross is the next person on screen.

'Shit.' I say as I pull my hand back from the tablet.

'No problem, it's touch sensitive. Just swipe in the other direction to bring it back.'

I hold my hands in the air, 'Not my thing, I'll leave that to you.'

As he moves the screen back to the video still I realise what is missing from the pictures.

'The hoods…the masks. They're not wearing any disguises. Are they all like this, the recorded streams, do they all show the faces of the victims?'

Luke nods. He also sits back down and draws the tablet back across the table.

ONE PIECE AT A TIME

'It is the general consensus the videos are the last recordings of the victims before death. We think that he doesn't care who sees them because they won't be around for much longer afterwards. He kills them when we see their faces.'

I think of Helen in the video. I can't believe I am hoping to see her in a next one still unrecognisable in a hood. I know if I see her face then it will be too late for us. Too late for her.

'Bring all your kit up to my office. JD needs to see this and we will want to see the US operation as well. I'll meet you there.'

I hurry over to the counter and order coffees and teas to go, JD will have to wait for his sandwiches but I grab a few Snickers and Mars bars to keep his sugar levels up.

Luke is already plugging his equipment into the plasma screen when I arrive holding the cardboard tray of hot drinks. Instead of a myriad of cables and wires I was expecting it takes just one HDMI lead from his tablet to the large screen. As I place the tray onto the table Luke takes out a mobile phone and starts swiping the small screen. I am just about to tell him to stop texting as we haven't got time when I see his movements are being replicated on the big screen. Each swipe or tap of his phone causes a corresponding movement or selection that we can all see. He sees my look and smiles at my lack of technological intelligence.

'Smartphone linked in to the tablet. Allows for smoother presentations and ease of use. I'll give you the program if you want.'

I plonk my phone on the table in front of him with a resounding thud.

'It's a phone,' I say. 'It takes phone calls and makes phone calls, and I can even manage to send a text now and again. What more do I need than that.'

Even JD rolls his eyes at my phone, an old Nokia that looks like it could do some damage if you hit someone with it,

'Give it up Luke, he's a techno heathen. He only carries a phone because he has to. He's more suited to the '70s with a whistle and a crap radio. All he needs is a dodgy 'tache and he could go right back in time like that 'Life on Mars' show and drive around in a Cortina.'

I smile. It's good to know that even in times of crisis that there is still humour about. When the dark comedy stops that is when I know we are really losing a case. I get hope from JD's comments, he hasn't given up hope on Helen yet so neither can I.

Graham picks up my phone and turns it around in his hands examining it,

'You know I should really have this on my examining table. The fact it is still in a working state is a miracle. Have you thought about donating it to science?'

'Or a museum.' Luke chirps in.

'All of you…just fuck off. It's my phone, it works and I don't need your shit.' I say good naturedly, 'Now give me that back before you drop it Doc. Your hands aren't as good as they used to be. JD, you can buy me a new phone for my birthday if you ever remember it and Luke…' I can't think of anything to say to the fresh faced, eager youngster, '…just get on with it.'

I bring JD and Graham up to speed with the facts given to me by Luke and we settle down to watch the show. Luke was right, they really know how to do things with technology in the states. I can see why he wants their budget because I wouldn't mind some of the hardware I see on screen as well.

CHAPTER 33

The unfolding events on screen are portrayed as nine separate squares of video footage all playing at the same time. Each has a small digital time stamp along the top of their respective picture showing they are all in sync.
'If you want to watch one or more of them bigger we can zoom in.' Luke says as he makes a small movement on his phone and the screen fills with just one picture. This shows an aerial shot from what I believe must be a helicopter. I recognise the grainy black and white image as a thermal camera and we see the white heat signatures of individuals as they move up to the side of the building.
Luke provides a commentary to the video before us.
'The UAV..' he looks at me, 'the unmanned aerial vehicle is providing an infrared feed. The white figures you see are the law enforcement officers preparing themselves to storm the building. This next bit is state of the art of tech.'
A line wipes across the picture in front of us and a 3D outline view of the building appears. At first I think it is a plan overlaid on the building but then I see people moving around inside.
'Is that an x-ray of the building?' I ask incredulously.
Luke taps again on the small screen and there are now two pictures on screen. The left side shows the view from above whilst the right side shows the view from the side.
'They have a ground unit bombarding the building with electromagnetic radiation, the aerial unit picks up the reflected waves and converts them into a 3D representation of the building. The IR feed also picks out the targets inside.'
He presses again and we go back to the aerial picture only. We can clearly see there are three people inside the building.
'How were they able to deploy so fast if we only asked for assistance yesterday?' I ask again.

Luke turns from the screen to face me.

'They have had this building and the men in it under surveillance for a while. There has been a huge amount of encrypted traffic being sent through their servers which the NSA, CIA and Homeland Security were attempting and failing to decipher. We offered to help them with their decryption if they could help us with our investigation. Apparently they were impressed that we have managed to get any information from these feeds as their guys have been at it for months and have gotten nowhere. They had been planning a raid for a few weeks and they just brought it forward when we explained our time-critical investigation.'

'Why have I not been informed of this?' JD is clearly angry with being shut out of the investigation. Luke doesn't know where to look so he stares at the screen,

'The commissioner has taken control of this side of the investigation. He has even gone over the head of Wilks and wants the responsibility of liaising with the Americans for himself.'

'You mean the glory and the limelight.' Says JD.

'He said he doesn't want any more fiascos like the last press conference. Sorry sir, his words, not mine.'

'No problem.' I say although my thoughts are thick with anger.

A bloom of white appears on screen.

'Ingress is achieved by a shaped charge on the door.'

We watch as many white figures charge the building, clearing rooms and making their way to the structure's core where two of the men are moving rapidly. One is motionless in the centre. Luke zooms in and I am amazed to see you can see his hands moving as though on a keyboard.

'It looks like he is erasing data from the servers. We are still awaiting confirmation on that as there was some damage to the hardware.'

'Can we see the other feeds.' I say.

Luke pans out the view and we see all the feeds available. The helmet or shoulder mounted cameras of the assault team are moving rapidly and we see in the aerial view when they reach the room where the three suspects are. On another screen we see hands holding a small, square lump of plastic explosive reach out to a steel door and knead it into position. The same hands place a small stick into the malleable material and back away. There is a bright flash of white on the aerial feed which corresponds with a large yellow flash and smoke from the assault team's cameras. Rapid movement as the team enters the room. We see one of the camera feeds pick up the flash of a weapon being fired then it is falling backwards and pointing at the ceiling, a fine red mist starts to form over the camera. Then all hell breaks loose. I wish there was audio so we could hear what was happening in all the confusion. Flashes from weapons seem to be everywhere. The assault team are firing into the smoke and I realise they must have infrared goggles on for them to be able to fire through the smoke. There is a huge flash of white and you see the cameras tumble as their owners stagger backwards. Luke interjects,

'Stun grenade. The men in the room were prepared. They also had automatic rifles and pistols with them. The stun grenade was used to disorient the assault team and damage their IR optics. They are firing blind now.'

The aerial view shows the multiple flashes from weapons all firing towards the location of the three men. The IR camera picks up the splashes as hits are made on the men and blood and gore goes flying in a fading white arc. It is all over in seconds.

Three figures lay sprawled in one area of the room whilst two of the assault team are motionless near the doorway. While help goes to the two law enforcement officers, two men move cautiously to the defenders of the room. There is a slight movement as one of the prone men moves an arm followed by a burst of light as a weapon is fired at him. I was too busy watching the aerial feed to see what happened on the point of view camera feed.

'My God.' Comes from Graham.

'What happened? Can we play that back?'

As the screen plays backward I see a weapon fall from the aim, 'OK that will do.' The video plays forward again.

I watch as the officer moves forward into the haze. His weapon barrel is pointing slightly downwards as he moves forward, not in the aim but in a state of readiness. There is movement in front of him. He raises the barrel into the aim. I see it is an arm raising itself towards him as if in surrender or asking for help. The barrel flashes as it barks out its deadly response and the arm drops suddenly. The camera pans around and you see the bodies in all their bloodied glory, twisted at angles that are impossible for living flesh to achieve. Behind them are racks of computer equipment and even through the smoke, even with the resolution of the camera, I can see that many of the computers have been seriously damaged by the brief battle.

The video stops.

'That was all that was transmitted to us, it stopped there just after the guy on the floor was shot but you can clearly see the damage to the server equipment was quite severe. As I said earlier, we are waiting on an assessment of the damage before we will know if it's possible to remove data from the drives.'

'What was the preliminary report of the intelligence found?' I ask Luke.

'It's with the commissioner. Like I said, he's running the show now.'

I stare at the blank screen not knowing what to think anymore.

CHAPTER 34

It is lucky, thinks Helen, that the two women have been dead for a while. What is it? she thinks to herself, three days, four? The coolness of the room has staved the smell off slightly but the real mercy is the small amount of blood that is spilt when removing the hands. Because the blood has pooled at the lowest point of the dead girls there is surprisingly little that spreads across the floor. She looks across at Zoe,
'Well done. It is hard work but you managed it. The legs and arms are worse, they take a lot more cutting and..'
'Shut up shut up shut up.' The shouting as it explodes from Zoe fills the small room with its noise.
'Just stop talking about it like it's normal. We just chopped the hands off two dead girls, we are covered in their blood and I am looking at their faces and wondering if I am going to be next.' She stares wildly at Helen and speaks more calmly, asking softly, 'Am I going to be next?'
Helen has to drop her gaze and her eyes focus on to the bucket on the floor with its gruesome contents. The water in the container has turned a dirty brown colour as the dead blood leeches from the veins and arteries of the hands and mixes with the clear fluid.
'I don't know.' Helen whispers, 'I just don't know. If you fight, you live. That is what he told me, the big guy with the Scottish accent that is. Not the other one who was killed yesterday, he was almost nice to us. He..'
'Nice…' spits out Zoe, '…he raped and abused both of us. He got what he deserved and I just wish he had not have died so quickly.'
'But he didn't know about the truth. I saw it in his eyes as he died, he was trying to apologise. I don't think he knew about the killings…I don't think he knew about us.'

ONE PIECE AT A TIME

Zoe laughs a cold, hard laugh, 'But he raped me. He raped me in front of that other man and he raped me in front of you…and he was filming it. For God's sake Helen, I nearly died because that fat bastard wanted the cameras off before he stopped me choking on my own vomit. I don't care if he died knowing about the deaths or not. He was part of it and he should have died for putting us and them,' she gestures towards the two corpses, 'through this. We are being kept like animals for their pleasure.'

The room falls silent as they each contemplate their fate and their immediate future.

Zoe picks up the gore covered knife.

'When he comes back I am going to kill him and you are going to help me. The two of us can do it if we work together. You fight, you know how to fight, let's fight him. Let's kill the bastard before he kills us.'

Helen thought she was the strong one but she is scared by the words coming from Zoe. If she fights and loses she is dead she thinks, but what is the guarantee she will survive this anyway. She only has the word of the Scottish man who told her only one would live and he killed his partner in these kidnappings. She raises her head.

'OK. You're right. If we don't get out now we never will. As soon as the door opens we rush him and start stabbing. Give me the knife.'

Zoe holds it close to her protectively. 'Why do you get the knife?'

Helen looks at the corpses behind her, 'I need it for a second then I will give it back. I need to make a weapon.' Then softly, 'Trust me.'

Zoe hands the knife over and moves back to her position next to the wall as Helen walks over to one of the bodies. She kneels down next to it and says, 'Sorry Bernadette, I have to do this.' Then starts sawing away at the elbow.

It only takes a few minutes for Helen to remove the forearm from the elbow. She scrapes away the flesh from the stump to reveal the glistening bone beneath. All this time Zoe has been staring on, at first in horror, and then as realisation hits her, in fascination. Using the serrated edge of the knife Helen starts to carve the flesh away from the bone until she has revealed around six inches of the hard white material. She dunks the exposed bone into the water bucket to swill away the gore clinging to it. Placing the forearm on the floor she smashes the hilt of knife into the ends of the bone, cracking and chipping flakes off. On the fourth hit a long jagged sliver breaks away and flies across the floor. Helen picks up the forearm and surveys her handiwork. Gripping the arm by the flesh near the wrist she now has a dangerous looking bone spike at one end. She hands the knife back to Zoe, 'That should do. Now we both have a weapon. The door opens, I will be on the left and go first. I will go for his face with this,' she waves the stump in front of her, 'and you will be low and right. Stab and slash him from the waist up. Maximum damage and aggression because if he doesn't go down straight away he will kill us.'

They move to their positions either side of the doorway and wait in the semi-darkness for the man to arrive.

CHAPTER 35

As I am thinking about the commissioner and his manipulation of the investigation, my phone, which is resting on the table still, starts to vibrate as a call comes through. I pick it up and answer before it continues its little dance on the hard surface. It is Julia.
'Peter, it's Dad he's woken up. I know you are tied up with your work but he won't speak to any other police. He said he will only talk to you about what happened to him. Can you come down to the hospital Peter? We need you. I need you. I love you.'
I look around the room at the faces before me and their silent expressions are similar to mine with the shock of the Commissioner's meddling with the case. There is nothing I can do here anyway.
'I love you too Julia. I'll be right there.'
She starts to say something else but I hang up the phone. I can't think straight with the maelstrom going on in my mind.
'Julia's father?' enquires JD.
I nod my head as I get my coat from the back of the door.
'Is he...?'
'No.' I say. 'He is awake and asking to speak only to me. He wants to tell me what happened to him.' I pause at the doorway. 'JD, we have to find out why the old man is taking such an interest in this. His interference could jeopardise everything so far. Contact Wilks and see what she knows and get uniforms out on the street looking for Stephens. Luke keep plugging away at the location of those camera feeds We find them, we find Helen and the other girls.' I turn back into the room to Graham as he holds up his hands.
'I have that hand to look at. The box and its contents may hold something we can use. Go and be with Julia and her father. We've got it from here Peter.'

I nod my thanks and walk silently from the office as they all watch my departure. I do not hear my office phone ring as I wearily make my way out. Graham answers it as he is nearest.

'DCI Carter's office.' He listens for a moment and shakes his head. 'OK, I'll let him know.' He hangs up the phone before looking at JD. 'There's another dismembered body been found. Only one hand has been left with it…with her. I'm betting it's a match for the hand we have already.'

JD faces the closed door and says, 'I hope it's not Helen.'

I get to the hospital quickly. It may have been a non-emergency but I used the blue light to clear the way. Bollocks to it, if they want to charge me with misuse of an emergency beacon then let them. I was willing and ready for a fight.

Julia meets me at the entrance and she is smiling and crying at the same time.

'Oh Peter, thank God. He's awake, he's going to be OK. The police officer outside the door tried to get him to speak about what happened but he refuses to talk to anyone but Stelios, Babis and you. He wants no one else in the room when he talks. Not even mama and me. But he's alive. I thought we had lost him.'

She buries herself into my chest and sobs with relief. I wrap my arms around her and hold her until she stops. I don't need to say anything, just be with her.

Nektarios is still covered in tubes and dressings. His hands are both wrapped up like huge balls of white candyfloss and his face is half covered in gauze. The bruising has really started to take hold and any exposed flesh is various depths of blacks and blues and browns. The one eye that is visible, watches me as I walk over to the bedside, and sparkles. The corner of his mouth rises slightly then grimaces with pain. His two brothers Stelios and Babis are also at his bedside looking both angry and curious at the same time.

'Peter, good to see you here so soon. Thank you.' Babis says.

I nod my head towards him. I don't feel I deserve his thanks with his brother lying in terrible pain before us.
'Anything for Nektarios.' I answer. 'Anything I can do to help I will.'
I sit down next to the bed and lean forward so that Nektarios does not need to struggle to make himself heard. The two brothers follow my lead and sit down also.
Nektarios' voice is soft and croaky but the strong, proud man speaks through the pain.
'Before I say anything I need you all to promise me you will do as I ask.' He turns his head slightly to his brothers, 'Especially you Babis. I need your word you will do as I say.'
I think back to how Babis wanted to bring his shotgun and hunt down the attackers and I feel a little worried. Babis nods his head, 'For vengeance I will swear to follow your words.'
Stelios nods also and says simply, 'I will follow your wishes.'
Nektarios turns to me, 'Peter. Will you do as I say? You are almost family now and we Cretans stick together. Can I trust you?'
'Nektarios,' I begin, 'if it is against the laws of this country I cannot do as you wish. But I promise to follow you and your brothers with all of my soul as far as I can. If that is not enough I will leave the room now so you can talk to your family, then I will come back alone to hear if there is anything you wish me to do…within the law.'
All that is heard in the room is the ticking of the clock in the background and the slow laboured breathing of Nektarios. The silence seems to drag on and I start to stand.
'I will come back in when your brothers leave the room.'
With what must be a supreme effort he raise his arm, 'No Peter. I do not wish you to go. I expect nothing less from a man of your integrity. Please sit.' He lowers his arm, 'Please.'
Both brothers are looking across at me intensely, I cannot read the expressions on their faces. It is like they have turned to stone.

'All of you have promised me. Thank you. Babis, Stelios…we know who did this. Peter, I must ask you not to persue this matter and I insist that Anna and Julia are not told anything.' He glares at me with his one good eye. 'I insist.'
I nod slowly my agreement.
'My attacker is a friend from long ago. My brothers know the story but you, Peter, need to hear it. Before I came to England I worked the fishing boats and olive groves with my brothers and father. He was in partnership with a man called Manolis from another family from our village, the Daskoulakis family. Anna was the daughter of Manolis. Our families did not know it but we were in love and wanted to get married. When we went to her father to ask for his permission he refused it saying that no daughter of his would be wed to a lowly fisher's son, even though that was what he was himself. He had already given his word that Anna would marry a man from Chania, a man I knew well. A man who was my friend. We were both stunned and shocked. I do not mind saying that I walked back to my family with tears in my eyes and my heart broken.'
He takes a deep breath as he recalls his past.
'My father met me as he was leaving to go hunting and naturally asked me what was wrong. When I told him what I had heard, he wanted to go straight to Anna's fathers with his shotgun and kill him, even though they had been friends since childhood. So much like you Babis, you are so much like him.'
I see Babis smile at the compliment.

'I managed to persuade him against that and said we should all sit down, me, him, Manolis and my friend to discuss the matter. He finally agreed but whatever we said we could not get Manolis or my old friend to do the same. Anna was such a beautiful woman, she had many admirers and my friend was no exception. He had always wanted her and knew that I was in love with Anna, but that just made him want her even more. I found out that in secret he had contacted Manolis and offered a huge dowry to have Anna as his wife, his family were politicos and had much land. They could afford it. Of course I felt betrayed by him, but I could also understand why Manolis took the offer. It meant a chance for him and his family to rise out of their hand to mouth existence and would support him into old age. It would also provide stability for future generations having Anna married into such a powerful family. Unfortunately for Manolis, Anna refused. She has always been a strong woman, that is why I fell in love with her. When my friend found out he confronted Anna, at first trying to sympathise with her and then threatening her. He lashed out and struck her whilst her father stood by and watched. This was too much even for Anna and as she looked to her father for help she felt her world collapse around her. A date was set for the wedding that night.'
I see tears bubble to the surface of his eyes and I lean across and wipe them from his cheek. He continues his story,
'I did not know about this until many years later when Anna finally told me. By then it was too late for me to do anything. We had made our life in England and I wanted no more vengeance.

The wedding was to be a huge affair with thousands of guests from all of Chania and Sfakia. The feasting began two days before the ceremony and would have continued long after it had I not intervened. I stole into Anna's bedroom the night before her wedding day and offered her my undying love if she ran away with me. If she did not do that I would leave anyway as I could not bear to see her with another man, especially a friend. We held each other and wept for hours and as dawn threatened to spill over the White Mountains she agreed to come with me. She knew the consequences for her. She knew she would never be able to see her father and mother again and that everything she knew and loved would be just memories from then on. But still she agreed to my wishes.

The day of the wedding we were already hidden away in the hills. I had stolen my father's motorbike and we escaped that morning with whatever possessions we could carry. I had some money from saving all year, and Anna had some money she had stolen from her father's desk. I found out years later there was nearly murder on our village streets that day as the three families clashed. Manolis blamed my father for helping us escape and my friend wanted to hunt Anna and myself down and kill us both for causing him and his family dishonour. He vowed to have my head on a plate while Anna watched before throwing her into the sea. Only the intervention of Anna's cousin, the priest conducting the ceremony, stopped killings happening that day. Blood was spilled as my father was shot in the arm by Manolis but that was the only blood that fell on the ground that day. From then on there was a feud between our families. Blood is sweeter when it falls from the flesh of an old friend and that was true for our families. We managed to escape Crete with the help of the same priest who had stopped the killings on her wedding day. He gave us enough money for a passage to Piraeus and from there I worked my way across Europe until we reached England. We married that same year and opened the restaurant the next, the year we had Julia. The feud roared and died like the flames of a fire, but our two families finally made peace when Manolis died two years ago. That is why Anna went back to Crete, after so many years she was finally able to go home and see her family, see her mother. What we did not count on was her slighted suitor, my friend, still bearing a grudge. He heard that Anna had returned to the village and called in to see her with his charming smile and fake sincerity. Luckily Babis was with Anna and saw through his deceit. Still, after all this time he now knew we were still alive and where we were. He came to me with his brother two days ago. He came to pay me back for the dishonour I bestowed upon him on his wedding day. That is how I ended up here like this.'

He faces his brothers.

'I want this to stop now. I do not want us to go back to the bad old days of everyone looking over their shoulder every time they hear footsteps. No more bloodshed. He has had his revenge and he must live with his actions. I must live with mine.' He turns painfully to me.

'Peter, I do not want to press charges. I want no action to be taken against this man and his family. This is a Cretan affair that has come to its rightful conclusion. No more is to be achieved by this. It stops here, in this room.'

I look at the two brothers and see the fury on their faces, but they both nod their agreement.

'Peter, there is one more thing. When you and Julia marry, I want it to be in our village in Crete. I want the wedding to take place in Spilia church where Anna and my friend should have married and I want him there. I want him to see the life we have had and the pleasure we have given each other. I want to see the look on his face when Anna and I watch our daughter get married in his church. That is my revenge for his actions. He cannot hurt our family any more. Peter I want you to invite my old friend, he is now the Mayor of Sfakia, to your wedding and I want him to see what he cannot have. You will have to visit him to get permission for the wedding, I want you to remind him of our friendship and what we once were. Tell him I forgive him.'

CHAPTER 36

The bright white tiles on the walls reflect the light from the powerful overhead lights so that hardly a shadow is made for the occupants of the tables. Moveable spotlights are also available at each metal table with extendable flexible necks for those times when more light is required on a certain spot. Graham does not think he will need to use those today. The eight foot long metal surface is raised and lowered by means of a hydraulic lift powered by a foot pedal. Graham pumps the pedal a few times to raise it to a more comfortable level for him to work on.

Before him, swamped by the vastness of the table, lies a hand and the open box it came in. The hand has already been fingerprinted and results will be forthcoming if a match is found but it is not like the CSI shows where everything happens in an hour. Fingerprint matches can easily take twenty-four hours or more to come through. He picks up a small yellow handled torch, the bulbs are placed centrally along the stem like a money forgery detector. In fact it uses the same principle of UV light to pick up unseen traces of evidence. Using a small remote control Graham dims the main lights and scans the hand for anything that might show up under the UV light. Semen, blood spots, hair fibres and many more almost invisible elements will shine brightly when exposed to the light. He is not expecting to find anything but it must be checked anyway. He carefully turns the hand over and checks both sides and between the fingers. Nothing. He moves to the small, moveable, metal tray used to hold the tools of his trade to put the torch down when he sees a luminescence from the box. The UV light has picked something out inside the lid of the box. Graham quickly moves back to the table and sweeps the box and lid.

The number 4 in a crude circle has been drawn inside the lid in some form of fluid that is invisible to the naked eye. Graham clicks on his digital recorder and starts to record his findings.

JD is standing on the Embankment looking over at the London Eye as it slowly turns above the river Thames. He doesn't see the appeal of it himself. Why pay all that money to stand in a glass bubble looking out over the city with dozens of others, all jostling to get to a window and take photographs of the same buildings over and over. He wonders if Shirley would like a trip on it, she might find it romantic. If she does that could get him some Brownie points even if he does find it ridiculous...like Mama Mia. He drags his gaze away from the huge metal structure back down to the black holdall resting against the small wall about fifty metres in front of him. Once again the bomb squad had been called out to investigate this suspicious looking bag dumped in a public area. A concerned passerby reported it, worried about another terrorist attack on the city. Since 7/7 there had been a heightened sense of self preservation amongst Londoners that the IRA failed to achieve with their bombing campaigns of the late 1990's. Now, if a bag was left alone for more than a few minutes there would be dozens of worried phone calls to the 999 emergency call room. Many were completely innocent but some, according to the NCA, were drops made by terrorist organisations to see how quickly a response team turned up to deal with it. The results varied widely according to which part of the city you were in. A package left outside the Houses of Parliament drew a response in minutes, whilst a bag dropped near an overpass of a busy road may go unnoticed and untouched for hours or even days.
JD watches as Gerwin and his team manoeuvre their robot back into their van.

'Hey big man, we must stop meeting like this. People will talk you know, I'm not one for bromances.' Gerwin's lilting accent booms out to JD even though he is standing only five feet away from him. He smiles.

'You're the one who is always chasing me I seem to think, Gerwin. I want a quiet walk along the riverside and you are already here to chat me up with your sweet patter. How come you're the one who is always called out anyway? Surely there is more than one team.'

'Luck of the draw mate, luck of the draw. Our shift was just about to end when the call came in. Ten more minutes and I would have been home on my settee watching Bargain Hunt with a nice cup of tea instead of stuck out here in the cold.' His face turns serious, 'This related to the other day and that Ripper thing going on?'

JD's mouth compresses into a thin line and he nods his head. 'We think so but this looks different to how other bodies have been found. They are normally left out of sight. This in full view is a new approach and I just hope it's not a copycat, we have enough on our plate as it is. What seems to match it up to the hand two days ago is the fact there is only one hand with the body parts in the bag. Again, that is different to the killers modus operandi, he usually puts...'

JD realises at the last minute he is about to share sensitive information that has not been released to the public. He stops talking abruptly and sees Gerwin smile sadly.

JD gets a tap on the back from the big Welshman, 'It must be tough to have to deal with this sort of thing. Try not to take it home with you but it's easier said than done. Believe me I know that you have to let it go somehow. For me, I use needlework. It relaxes the mind and gives your hands something to do when you want to reach for another bottle.'

'Needlework?' JD asks surprised.

'Try it...don't laugh. Just give it a go, I guarantee you will be pleasantly surprised.'

Now that the bag has been cleared by the bomb squad the forensic technicians are able to start their job properly. A small screen has been erected during their conversation and protects the vital work that the forensics team do from prying eyes and the elements. The one hundred metre cordon will be swept inch by inch for any clues that may have been inadvertently dropped along with the holdall and JD must wait patiently for a path to be cleared before he can enter the exclusion zone.

'Right then. With a bit of luck I can get back to barracks, fill out the report and get home in time for Countdown.' Gerwin holds out his hand to JD. 'Needlework, remember that. Take it easy and see you around.'

JD squeezes the bomb disposal sergeant's hand, 'Thanks again for your help. Enjoy your Countdown.'

Gerwin turns back to his truck and says as a goodbye, 'Not the same since Carol left.'

JD pulls out his phone and calls Graham but gets no answer and has to leave a message on his voicemail.

'Graham, we will be at least another hour before we bring this one in. I hope you can give this your priority and start work straight away. I'll call you when the body is on its way and it will be coming directly to you.'

Graham hears his phone ringing on the counter top but is in the middle of carefully disassembling the small box. Scrapings of the material where the number 4 was drawn have already been sent off for analysis and now Graham is examining the box and using thin scalpel blades to peel away the layers of paper and cardboard that it is constructed from. A stronger UV light has been wheeled over so that Graham can use both hands to work on the evidence in front of him. He presses the blade into the left corner crease at the back of the box, slicing down smoothly along the corner. A glint of blue from the UV appears as the box folds open and Graham is upon it instantly with his tweezers. He holds it up to the light to examine it…a human hair. Dark, thick and definitely not from the straw coloured hair that sparsely populates the hand on the table in front of him. He smiles as he places the tiny hair into a sterile test tube. Now all we need, he thinks, is something to DNA match it with and we have a suspect.

CHAPTER 37

Luke is desperate to go to the toilet. He must have had about eight cups of coffee since the playback of the assault in the DCI's office just over two hours ago and now all that fluid wants to get out of his body.
'One more minute.' He tells his heavy bladder as he squirms a little uncomfortably in his seat.
The information on his screen is broken into two parts, the bottom half shows a list of IP addresses which are being highlighted one by one. As each changes from black to yellow the top half of the screen shows a thin red line tracing from one location to another on a computer generated map layout. If Luke were to zoom out the traced lines would show a messy web that intersect almost every country in the world. This is how the TOR system works, constantly jumping from one location to another as the data is fed through the network. Luke has managed to write a short program that circumnavigates part of the security features of the TOR system. This is the program that the Americans want from him as it will allow greater traceability of illegal data start and end points. What Luke is waiting for is the trace line to stop. What he is waiting for is the last IP address of the live camera feed that showed Helen Carter and the unidentified girl being abused yesterday.
He can't wait a minute longer, his legs are pressed together and he is almost doubled over with the pain in his bladder.

'Shit.' He mutters as he gets up from his workstation to make his way to the toilets at the end of the corridor. The door closes automatically behind him just as the monitor stops its movement. A single line of numbers is displayed on the bottom half of Luke's screen and the map has frozen in place. The thin red line has stopped and is terminated in a flashing circle showing an area near the bank of the river Thames near the Dartford crossing. In bold capital letters across the centre of the screen two words flash slowly.
'SOURCE IDENTIFIED'

Commissioner Derek Temple is in a hurry. He has a meeting with the Mayor of London and the US ambassador this afternoon who both want details of the investigation and the subsequent co-operation of the Metropolitan Computer Forensics Unit with their TOR decryption program, with Luke's decryption program to be exact. Officially, as Luke has written it personally and not used any of the Met's resources, it is up to him whether he shares the information and what remuneration package is wanted. Derek Temple is coming down to see him to persuade the young man that full disclosure would be good for the young man's career…as well as his own of course. If he can talk Luke into giving away the program to the Yanks then Derek is sure a knighthood would be coming his way in the New Year Honours list. Sir Derek…no that's not good. Lord Temple…yes that works out better. He repeats it in his mind a few times and smiles at the sound of it in his head. He opens the door to the computer labs and makes his way inside as he imagines himself in front of the Queen on one knee. He walks purposefully towards Luke's desk and shakes his head at the clutter of empty coffee cups and chocolate wrappers that adorn his desk. His eyes are drawn to the computer screen and its simple flashing message. He leans over the desk for a better look and realises what he is looking at. He smiles as it dawns on him that his knighthood is virtually guaranteed with the information before him. He takes a careful note of the location of the feed on the map before moving his hand across the desk and manoeuvring the mouse. He moves the cursor to the task bar at the top of the screen and hovers over a small dialog box there. He looks around the room but the only person who is present is too intent on his own computer screen to even be aware that the commissioner is in the room. He presses the left mouse button and the box highlights for a brief moment, 'Repeat Trace Started'. The screen once again starts filling slowly with strings of numbers and a thin red line makes its way across the computer generated map. Derek stands up straight and turns to leave just as Luke walks in from his toilet break.

'Ah…just the man I wanted to see. Have you decided on the actions for the TOR decryption with our American friends yet?' He asks.

Luke is slightly bewildered to see the commissioner at his desk.

'Uh…it's not that simple sir. The program is still in testing stages as you can see on my screen. I was hoping to have managed to traced something…anything by now but there appears to be a glitch in the program somewhere. It should have bounced the false IP addresses and cross referred the real ones against the MAC codes for identified machines which would enable it to….'

'Stop there son, you've lost me at IP. If it works will you share it with other agencies is all I need to know?'

'Sir, if it helps to stop criminal activity yes,' Luke pauses as he thinks about his next words, 'But I would need guarantees about its uses. TOR was built to protect individuals against oppressive and unjust censorship from regimes that want to stop free speech. This program could have far reaching repercussions…sir, people could die because of it.'

Derek nods his head as if deep in thought,

'I understand your reluctance but you need to think of the bigger picture and also your own future.' He looks sternly at the young man before him, 'I am sure you will do what is right.'

Derek Temple, commissioner of the London Metropolitan Police Force, walks away with thoughts of his own future filling his mind. Luke shakes his head as he watches the older man walk away, 'You just don't get it do you?' he whispers to himself as he turns and watches the numbers snake down the screen in front of him.

'You just don't understand the consequences.'

Outside the room, Derek pulls out his phone and makes a quick call.

'Awfully sorry Gina, I will have to cancel my two 'o'clock with the mayor. Let him know there will be a press conference at three with a breakthrough in our investigation. I cannot say more over the phone.'

He hangs up and redials another number,

'Sean, I need discretion. I want an armed response unit available for me in ten minutes waiting and ready to go…No, just five men will do…That's right, ten minutes. I will brief them on the way…Thank you Sean, you know I won't forget this help.'

He strides back to his office oblivious of the people around him. This is his time for glory and by God he is going to make sure that the world sees him centre stage.

In his office he opens the small wardrobe and pulls out his protective vest which he puts on under his jacket. Going to the small safe on the far wall he punches in the code to the digital lock and pulls it open. Taking out the Glock 17 9mm pistol he checks the chamber is empty before inserting a magazine into the handle. He clips the pistol into its hard plastic holster and attaches it to his belt along with a spare magazine. He wants to be ready for anything that may come his way. He catches sight of himself in the mirror next to his door and pulls the waterproof jacket over the holster. He doesn't want to look like a cowboy as he breaks the story of the year to the press later on. He picks his peaked cap from the hook on the back of the door and checks himself once more in the mirror.

'Arise Lord Temple,' he mutters to his reflection. He smiles thinly, pulls himself erect and leaves his office.

CHAPTER 38

Julia and Anna both look over expectantly as Stelios, Babis and I leave the hospital room. Babis moves over to Anna and starts talking in low tones with her. Stelios looks at me and Julia and says, 'I will get some coffee for us all.' and walks away down the sterile corridor. I move towards Julia.
'What did he say Peter? Does he know his attackers?'
I wrap my arms around her, 'It's complicated.' I say as I bend down to kiss her. As I pull my lips from hers I look at her beautiful face, 'He has given us his blessing for our marriage and he wants us to get married in Crete, in your parent's old village.'
Tears spring to her eyes, 'We can't. It's too dangerous for them to return. Mama told me why they had to leave, why it has taken so long for her to go back and why I have never been. I am sorry I never told you, it was a personal thing for them.'
Nektarios you old fool, I think, your family knows everything. I stroke her hair as I kiss her again.
'Your father, he told me everything Julia. The wedding, the elopement, coming to England and the full story about Anna and his old friend. He says it stops here, no more bloodshed, no more vengeance. He wants to move on and he wants our marriage to show the families that life must go on with happiness instead of fear and reprisals. I promised to do what he said but I will go back on my word if you do not want the same. I will marry you wherever you want, however you want and whenever you want. I love you, Julia, and that means I love your family too, but you come first. You.'
Her reply is to kiss me and hold me even tighter in her fragile arms.

Stelios interrupts our thoughts, 'It is settled then.' he says as he hands over two cardboard cups of cheap vending machine coffee. 'I shall arrange the wedding and celebrations for you. You will pay nothing, it is my honour to do this for the return of my brother.'
Babis walks over with Anna in tow, 'For our brother, *we* shall pay for everything.'
He punches Stelios playfully on the shoulder causing a small amount of hot liquid to be spilled on the shining vinyl floor.
'It will be like old times again, eh Stelios?'
'Stop that.' The harsh voice of one of the nurses causes us all to turn around in her direction. 'Stop that spillage, this is a hospital not a damn cafeteria. Move on into the waiting room or get out, but remove yourselves from my corridor.'
Stelios and Babis smile to each other and Stelios turns to Anna,
'She must be Greek, she sounds just like our Mama.'

In the waiting room we are sat around discussing the wedding and Nektarios' health when my phone rings in my pocket.
'DCI Carter.'
'Peter, we have an interesting development down here.' Graham's voice brings me back to the present with a chill, ' Any chance you can pop in to my office to discuss it. JD is out bringing in the latest victim, Superintendent Wilks has been called into an urgent last second meeting with the Mayor and nobody is able to say where the Commissioner is at the moment. So I thought of you.'
'OK Graham.' I check my watch, 'I will be there within the hour. Can you say what it is over this line?'
'We have a DNA match between some evidence from yesterday and a deceased male that I worked on a few days ago. I think he has been involved in the kidnappings.'
Helen's bite marks I think immediately, 'I will be there soon Graham. Thanks for letting me know.'

As he says, 'No problem.' I am already hanging up the phone. All faces are looking at me as they have heard the excitement in my voice on the phone.

'I have to go. I am sorry it has to be like this, but…'

'No need to explain Peter. You must do what you have to. Please, we will be alright here. We have much to discuss and arrange.'

Anna's words are finished with a huge, loving smile to her daughter. I look at the family in front of me, reunited against all odds after a brutal act of violence that has been implemented by a thirty-year-old feud, and I feel hope. I throw my coffee into the waste bin and head out of the door.

It takes me thirty long minutes to get to Grahams office and as I walk in he is typing away on his computer whilst cradling his phone to his ear. He holds up one hand as I enter and I sit down at what is supposedly my desk in his huge office and wait for him to finish.

'I understand your reluctance to release provisional findings Matt, but this is of a time critical importance…yes I know it is your name on the header…yes…yes…look, please just hurry it through.'

He types away angrily on his keyboard and I feel sorry for the black keys in front of him.

'I...' smash, 'do...' smash, 'not...' SMASH, 'care.' He pushes the keyboard away and grasps the phone from his neck. 'Matt, get the results to me in the next hour. People could die because of your reluctance and you are worried about it not being proofread and approved by your boss...shut up...I am speaking now. As far as you are concerned I am your boss at this moment in time. I will take any and all responsibility for any inaccuracies in the data you provide, you will not be implicated if there is a board of inquiry and you and your team will only get the praise, but I swear if I do not get that report on my desk before 1pm I will be ripping you a new hole for you to defecate from and then you will be looking for a new job. Am I making myself clear?...Good.'
Graham slams the phone down and misses the cradle, instead hitting the speakerphone button.
'What a fucking arsehole.' Booms out from the loudspeaker before the line goes dead.
I look up at a shocked Graham's face and burst out laughing.
'You know how to make friends, don't you.' I state.
He looks grimly back at me,
'Peter, if only you knew. I have a basic DNA match between this,' he holds up a small glass tube, 'and this gentleman.' He points to his screen where I can see he has been typing up an autopsy report. 'I have requested a DNA check against our records and received an e-mail saying a match had been returned. I have just been trying to get that information but Matt in profiling is such a damn jobsworth. He needs an operation to get his head out from his arse.'
He finally moves the phone into the cradle correctly.
He turns the glass test tube in his hands.

'This hair was found in the box that the hand was delivered in yesterday. It matches this victim of a slashed throat I was called to two days ago. I don't need to tell you it is more than just a coincidence that the DNA matches from two seemingly unconnected cases. This man is undeniably linked in with the kidnappings, murders and mutilations of at least five women we are aware of and I want to know how. I want to know everything about him and I want it yesterday but some people are too pre-occupied with their own reputations to give a toss about anyone else.'

I look steadily at him, 'Rant over?' I ask.

He stares back and sighs deeply, 'Rant over.' He agrees.

'Now tell me what you've got and what our next steps are.'

I listen intently for the next ten minutes as he describes his findings, so intently I do not hear the door open behind me or the person enter the room until they speak.

'Gentlemen, we have a situation.'

CHAPTER 39

A stray dog wanders along the road and makes a beeline towards a line of rubbish dumped against the back wall of the building. Derek Temple watches from the driver's seat, uncomfortable in his stab vest, as the dog noses through the abandoned bags before pawing curiously at one of them. The dog manages to rip one of the bags open and his snout pushes through the gap made before it pulls away triumphantly with a prize. It slopes away with whatever tasty morsel it has discovered and disappears around the corner.

Derek surveys the area around him from the car. He is surrounded by nondescript warehouse buildings and overflowing rubbish bins of all types of industrial and normal waste. A cheap looking health club stands on the corner, its windows lit up from within as its occupants sweat and strain using the equipment inside. The top floor windows are flanked by tables and he can see people milling about inside. Probably enjoying one of those god-awful yoghurt drinks his wife keeps trying to get him to have every morning, he thinks. The tap on the window brings him back to the present.

'Sir there is only one entrance into the building and the door there, is the only other exit. It looks like a standard building but we have no way of knowing the layout inside. I propose we call for assistance and perform a full assault in two teams of ten from both sides.'

Derek shakes his head.

'We go in with what we have. I want two of your men stationed at the rear door in case of runners whilst we go in as two teams of two and sweep the building.'

'With all due respect sir it's a big building. Without knowing the layout, the number of people inside, if they have any weapons...hell, any intelligence would be better than what we have...'

'Your considerations are noted but we do it my way. When I was in charge of the ARU's my men listened to their commander and trusted him. Do you trust me Sergeant?'
'Yes sir, I just wanted to let you know my thoughts on an alternative…'
Derek interrupts him, 'Noted. Now two men to the rear door and the rest of you follow me.'
The plain clothes sergeant points to two of his unit and directs them to the emergency exit with hand signals. He walks over to his unmarked car and opens the boot to reveal an arsenal of weapons all strapped in neatly to every available surface. Derek follows him and smiles when he sees the Franchi Spa semi automatic 12 gauge shotgun. He reaches in and plucks it from its Velcro strapping ensuring it is fully loaded and the five shotgun shells attached to the butt are secure in their elastic webbing..
'I'll take this.' he tells the officers.
The other officers reach in and take their weapons, a H&K MP5 submachine gun each and pistols for close range work. The MP5 is a superb weapon for urban use, its short barrel allows for easy manoeuvrability in confined spaces and its subsonic 9mm round will not penetrate walls to inflict unwanted casualties.
Derek turns to the men,
'We are looking for at least one hostile male, possibly more. There are two live hostages that we can be sure of with the possibility of more. Some may be injured. Be on your toes and keep alert. You know your rules of engagement so only fire if fired upon or if there is immediate threat of death or serious injury to you or anyone else.'
He takes off his peaked cap and throws it in the back of the car. 'Let's go.'
The other officers all remove the Velcro patch on the front of their jackets to show the 'POLICE' badge beneath it and follow the commissioner towards the building.

Derek motions for one of his men to go forward and try the door. If it is locked they will have to use the ram to forcefully gain entrance but the door swings outward easily. He nods and the four men step quietly inside the doorway.

The entrance is a corridor of painted breeze blocks with three internal doors leading off it, one on either side and one at the far end. Derek is just about to split his team up to check the doors either side of the corridor when the door in front of them opens.

A large man steps through and stares at the four men in front of him. For a brief second no-one moves, so complete is the shock of the meeting.

'Armed police, stay where you are.' Derek shouts.

The figure turns swiftly for a man of his size and slams the door shut behind him.

Rushing forward, Derek yanks the door open to allow his team access and follows them through into a large warehouse room. Their suspect has disappeared amongst the racks and shelving that line the room in long rows and the only sound that can be heard is the hum of electrical equipment as it reverberates around the large area. Derek raises two fingers and points to the left hand side of the room. Two of his men peel away and start to move slowly forward, weapons in the shoulder as they do so. He turns to the officer next to him and mouths 'on me'. The officer nods and gives a thumbs up in acknowledgement and follows his commander into the dimly lit area. They hear a door slam shut ahead and resist the urge to rush forward to the sound.

'Did you hear that?' Zoe whispers to Helen. 'He's here.'
Helen grips her gruesome weapon in front of her and whispers back, 'Be ready, we will only get one chance.'
They both wait there in the darkness in frightened anticipation for the door to open so they can attack. The sounds from outside increase as doors are opened and slammed shut and they hear muffled curses from the room beyond.

The sound of the dead bolt drawing across makes them both grip their respective weapons tighter. Helen is sweating, even in the coolness of the dark room, and she feels her hands slipping on the cold skin she holds so tightly. She wipes one hand on her thigh in an attempt to dry her hands which helps slightly. She sees Zoe tense herself as the door bolt snaps back into its open position with a dull metallic thud.
'One chance.' Helen repeats.
Zoe flicks her eyes over to her. Helen wonders what she must look like to Zoe, standing there in the semi-darkness, naked and holding a splintered forearm as a weapon. The door opens slowly, cautiously. Helen grabs the opening rim of the door and yanks it forward, inward towards her and screams as loud as she can, 'NOW'.
They both rush the man who is framed in the light, hacking, stabbing, slashing as he falls backwards under their frenzied attack.

Derek and his team have worked their way though the warehouse storeroom and are now poised at the only door in the room. They passed two bricked up doorways, one still retaining its frame before they reached this heavy looking metal, sliding, double width door. Luckily there does not seem to be any lock on that is fitted integrally to the door itself, but it could be chained or secured somehow on the other side. If it is Derek knows he will have to call in support and they will have a siege with hostage situation. He holds his breath as one of his team places his gloved hands out and pulls the handle on the door. His sigh of relief is loud as the door rolls smoothly along its track and opens up the area beyond. He moves into the room with his shotgun held in front of him. Just like the old days, he thinks.

The place is full of computer equipment. Blinking red and green lights flash in random sequences against the web of green, yellow, red and grey cabling that criss-crosses the whole room just above head height. It is like a Salvador Dali interpretation of a mechanical spiders lair.

They move forward as a group, spread as wide as possible within the confines of the room to prevent being one large target for any would be attacker. Derek leading from the front sees the man at the computer terminal before the others.

'Armed police…Stop what you are doing and raise your hands in the air.'

The man barely glances in his direction and Derek repeats himself, even louder this time,

'ARMED POLICE, PUT YOUR HANDS IN THE AIR…NOW.'

This time the figure who is being illuminated by the soft glow of the computer screen does not even manage a glance towards the armed figures. Instead he types even more rapidly at the keyboard in front of him, the keys clacking away like a tuneless xylophone. Derek chambers a round in the shotgun, the sound is loud enough and threatening enough, to make the man at the computer pause and look up.

'I am not armed.' he states in his thick accent as he stares straight down the shotgun barrel, his fingers barely slow their tap tapping on the keyboard. He raises his right hand as if to show he has no weapon, smiles, then drops it down on the 'Enter' key.

There is a popping sound to Derek's right and he turns, startled, in time to see the lights go out on the computer equipment on the racks and puffs of smoke emerge from the back of the metal boxes there. He turns back to face the man in front of him,

'What have you done?'

The man smiles and states again as he raises his hands, 'I am not armed.'

He looks to one side, the smile still on his face, 'But they are.'

All hell breaks loose in the warehouse as Derek and his Armed Response Unit come under fire.

Across the small road and sitting in the gym's small café, two men sit with a cup of coffee each and listen to the tinny, small pops of the weapon explosions coming from the warehouse opposite. A bearded man with a soft Aberdonian accent turns to his companion and shakes his head,
'So that's the Pakistanis in the US sorted and the Bosnians here. You really know how to increase the profit margins don't you. I may have to watch my back or you will be after my share too.'
He smiles as he takes a sip of the insipid brown liquid.
Neal Stephens does not smile back as he looks at his companion across the table.
'You don't need to worry about that Jim. I need you to keep finding the girls, and there's always more girls aren't there.'
He raises his own cup and clinks it against the other opposite him, 'Here's to another successful year next year…here's to Vegas.'
They both flinch instinctively as a huge explosion blasts through the building opposite. Stephens has just enough time to turn and see the roof lift as if pushed up by an invisible hand, before it settles back on to its walls and then slowly collapse into itself. The blast cracks the windows in the gym's cafeteria, but since the IRA bombings and the more recent terrorist attacks on London, the windows have been treated with clear blast film to prevent splintering in just such an incident. Stephens knew this and that is why he was not worried overly about the explosion. He would have to write a report for his company about the effectiveness of the material, because after all, it was his company that installed it.
'Fuck me!' his partner exclaims, 'That was unexpected.'
Stephen's smiles slowly as he takes a sip from his cup, 'Hmmm, wasn't it.'

CHAPTER 40

'When did this happen? Who authorised the use of an ARU?' Wilks is still standing just inside the doorway as I throw my questions at her. She has a look of shock on her face that has not changed from when she entered and told us about the situation in Dartford.

'The explosion occurred around twenty minutes ago. We believe at this time that the Commissioner authorised it and was perhaps on the mission with them. It is thought he is one of the victims of the explosion, but, we are waiting for the remaining survivor of the ARU to regain consciousness before we know the full details of the operation. Sean Johns, the head of the ARU, has told us that the commissioner wanted a squad of the Armed Unit to be at his disposal. Nothing was put in writing, as far as Sean is concerned he was following orders of the commissioner. I'm not sure if you know but Derek got Sean the job as ARU chief after they worked together on the unit many years ago, there is loyalty there.' She huffs out a breath, 'Huh, loyalty. Derek's bloody keyword.'

'How did the officer survive the explosion.' I ask.

'He and a colleague were outside the rear entrance. His oppo was hit by a large piece of the metal door as the explosion blew. She didn't stand a chance, poor girl. The blast through the doorway looks like it picked our man off his feet and slammed him into the wall across the alleyway about thirty feet away. He's in a bad way but his condition is serious but stable according to the medics.' She pauses, runs her fingers through her hair and takes a deep breath, 'But we all know that stable means they can't do anything to help. We are not sure if he will make it through the night.'

'Who owned the warehouse?' I ask.

'Unknown at this time.'

'What about its purpose?'
'Unknown.'
'Apart from the ARU, how many involved?'
'Unknown until the wreckage is cleared. We know for a fact there were five members of the ARU and we can only surmise the commissioner was with them as we cannot contact him through any channels. As you can imagine his wife is distraught.'
'Do we think our kidnap victims were in the building? Was this an operation in our investigation?' I try not to think of Helen's body ripped apart and buried beneath a pile of mangled concrete and iron.
'Unknown.'
That is not the answer I wanted.

Luke is in a half dozing state as he watches, mesmerised at the numbers cross the screen in front of him. His mind, he has told himself many times and also in explanation to his colleague, works better that way. He tells them it soaks in the information and sees and analyses patterns that his conscious mind drifts over. He knows they just think he is daydreaming on company time but it does prove effective.
He suddenly sits bolt upright in his high backed chair. He taps a few commands into the keyboard. There, he types a few more commands, there again. He runs a quick test and sees a set of numbers appear on the screen once again. It is not an anomaly of the system. He inputs a command to slow the results down and sees it properly, his daydreaming has spotted a pattern which he would probably have missed was he fully concentrating. The same IP address has kept repeating itself for the briefest of instants during the trace. He calls up the number on his screen and runs a trace. His eyes widen as he sees the location appear on screen.
'Bloody hell.' he whispers to the glowing square in front of him, 'You're just around the corner.'

He picks up the phone and hits the speed dial button. The phone on the other end rings a few times and goes through to an answer-phone.

'Ma'am, it's Luke. I have an address that looks promising. I will check it out and get back to you.'

He reels off the location and hangs up. Grabbing his jacket he hurries out of his offices and out into the real world.

Twenty five minutes later, Luke is standing in an area of London that is undergoing redevelopment. A huge billboard proclaims 'Welcome to the new home of Allied Honour Security Systems. A proud new development by Windsor Industries.'

Situated on the bank of the Thames in an area that has, up until now, been overlooked by the developers of multi-million pound apartment complexes, it is full of abandoned warehouses and half-demolished buildings. Luke remembers the site as being some form of government funded chemical plant. Maybe the clear up operation was too costly for many companies to pursue, but with land in London so scarce it was only a matter of time before the prices became viable for profit.

Luke knows about this place because he grew up about two hundred yards away in the crammed together terraced houses that now look even more decrepit than they did when he was younger. In fact as a ten or eleven year old he used to play with his friends in and around the area of waste ground he now stands on, fifteen years later. He moves purposely towards the largest of the buildings still intact.

'Just a quick look,' he tells himself aloud as he walks across the broken ground, 'I'll take a quick look inside and if I see anything it's straight back to the office and get Carter.' He chuckles, 'Get Carter. I like it. Wonder how many times he's heard that one?'

Figuring the door to the building is probably locked, he clambers up a dangerous looking fire escape ladder and gains entry through a broken window.

'Just like old times,' he thinks to himself as he puts his feet down onto the dusty concrete walkway that rims the interior of the warehouse. The light from the window only illuminates a few feet either side of the frame. Luke gives his eyes a few seconds to let his eyes grow used to the darkness and treads forward carefully. Ten steps in and he can't see a thing. He fumbles in his pocket for his phone and activates the torch function. The stark white light punches its narrow beam through the darkness and at least allows him to see the crumbling floor beneath his feet.

He pauses high up on the walkway as he hears a noise up ahead. He strains his eyes trying to peer through the darkness, his phone pressed into his chest to avoid giving away his position. Hearing nothing more he moves slowly forward again, his light picking obstacles of fallen concrete and holes in the walkway that show black holes into the depths below.

He reaches the set of stairs he remembers from his youth. A solid flight of metal steps that lead down onto the ground floor.

'At least they used to be solid.' he says out loud. He looks around in the darkness wondering if he has made a mistake. There is obviously nothing here, the huge warehouse is empty and black, but the offices are at the back, he thinks. There could be something there.

Cursing himself for his local knowledge he begins his descent downwards. The stairs are as solid as he remembers and he breathes a sigh of relief as makes his way downward to touch down onto the concrete floor. He stops to get his bearings for a second before heading off in the direction of where he thinks the offices were. He is only a few feet off as his torch picks out the frame of the large entrance doorway just off to his left. Walking into this smaller room he walks confidently forward to the location of the door in front of him. He shines his light around the door frame before bringing it to rest on the round handle in front of him. Pressing his ear against the wooden door he hears nothing but the thud of his own heartbeat as it pounds blood though his body.
'In for a penny...'
He reaches one hand out, turns the door knob and pushes the door open.

Superintendent Wilks is back in her office trying to piece together the events of the morning. She has been so busy fielding phones calls, from the mayor's office down to the army of press hounds, that she has not registered the small blinking red light indicating she has waiting messages. She is in the middle of drafting a press release when I walk in.
'Any more news?' I ask.
She shakes her head, 'Only bad news I'm afraid. The officer who survived the explosion died a few minutes ago.'
She places her pen down on her table.
'Six officers lost, one of which is the commissioner of the Met. It is the worst day for the force in living history and I have to deal with it without yet knowing the full facts behind an operation I should have been in full awareness of. I have to explain that to the families of six brave people who died today. I have to tell them I don't know why they died because my superior officer decided to walk out of the door without explaining his actions. I can say he was a glory chasing bastard, but that will not console anyone but me.'

'He had his reasons,' I say, 'he may not have shared them but, he was a damn fine copper in his day and…'

'Six people are dead because of him, Peter. For Christ's sake, he took four men and one woman to their deaths today and you are defending him.'

I move forward towards her, 'He didn't kill them, he was doing what he thought was right, no matter what the misguided reasoning. Glory, awards, fame…who cares. He was doing his job and moving forward but circumstances got the better of him and he made a wrong call. They were killed by the people in that building, not by him…he didn't pull a trigger or blow up a bomb. No-one could have foreseen that, in fact, if more people were on the job it is likely that more would have died or been seriously injured. Be thankful for that.'

She quickly and delicately wipes her eyes with a fingertip. 'Thank you Peter. You're right. In all this mess I suppose there is something we should be thankful for.'

She straightens behind her desk.

'What's happening downstairs? Have you heard word if they have found anyone in the rubble yet?'

I shake my head. 'JD is on scene with half the force looking for answers. If this is related to our investigation he is the man to be there. I…I am not sure I should be with my personal involvement in the case.'

'If it is part of our operation and Helen and the other girls are there, well, there could still be survivors, don't give up hope.'

'It's the only thing I have left.' I reply as I turn to leave her office. 'I'll be in Graham's office if you need me. He's waiting for news of victim identification. He's going to have a long few days ahead of him.'

Wilks watches as Carter leaves the room, head bowed and already looking broken by the thought his sister is dead. She shakes her head slightly and picks up her pen. It is then she notices the flashing red light on her phone. Thinking it will be another pointless message asking for details she hits the play button with a deep sigh in preparation. The message played back makes her hold her breath as Luke's information is replayed.
'PETER…GET BACK IN HERE,' she shouts loudly to the open door.

CHAPTER 41

Neal Stephens is following the big man back to the warehouse. At times he cannot hold back his disdain for the man in front of him and now is one of those times. It takes all of Stephen's willpower not to take the folding Applegate Gerber combat knife from his belt loop and plunge it into the man's neck in front of him.
'Fucking oxygen stealer.' he mouths silently.
The big man stops and turns around, 'Huh, what was that?'
'Didn't say a word mate.'
'Oh.'
They continue walking.

Back in Iraq, Stephens had met Jim Barnwell during an operation to arrest a local Iraqi henchman. Jim was much leaner and tougher then, but he was still a vicious bastard. On entering the house they had found the suspect without much trouble and he had given himself up quite easily. While he was being led away by the regular RMP team to the vehicle, Barnwell and Stephens were tasked with searching the upper floor of the small house. Stephens had followed Barnwell into one of the spartan bedrooms and was amazed when his partner went straight to a rug and whipped it away to reveal a trapdoor hidden beneath it like he knew it was there.
Barnwell placed his fingers to his lips and pointed his weapon at the hidden door.
'Harish… Harish… Out…Out' he shouted as foot stomped on the wood beneath it.

Slowly, the trapdoor opened to reveal a young woman, no more than sixteen or seventeen, hiding inside. She was lying on a bed of American dollars and Barnwell's eyes widened as he saw the bounty in front of him. He turned to Stephens whose reaction was also to stare helplessly at the treasure in front of him.

'Fuck me.' Stephens exclaimed.

The two men exchanged glances and they see the greed in each other's eyes.

'We could…' Barnwell says

Stephens nodded and turned to look at the stairwell behind them.

'Go and head off the guys and get your pack, your Bergen, from the Wolf.' Barnwell instructed him.

Stephens recalls how he told the team to get the suspect back as fast as they could in the Snatch Land Rover with the Mastiff as support, leaving two men and another wagon with the mounted General Purpose Machine Gun, GPMG, as support whilst the search continued. He instructed the two soldiers to wait outside and keep the perimeter secured while they completed the search. Grabbing his Bergen he then hurried back inside the building.

Entering the bedroom again, he found Barnwell on top of the Iraqi girl, viciously pounding his body into hers. Her mouth was stuffed with a pillowcase from the bed to stop her screaming and he saw her eyes were streaming with tears as her body was abused.

'What the fuck are you doing?' he spat out at Barnwell.

The other man raised his face and just grinned whilst still pumping away.

'Having a little fun man, just having a little fun.'

Stephens made to move forward but stopped as a pistol was raised to his face.

'Don't even think about it.'

Stephens was frozen as he looked down the dark barrel of the Browing Hi-Power 9mm pistol. It seemed the next few seconds moved as if in slow motion. Barnwell started to speed up his thrusting into the girl and she looked up into Stephens' eyes, pleading silently with him to stop her abuse. He watched helplessly as the pistol moved from being pointed at him to being pressed against the temple of the girl. Her eyes widened even more as she felt the greasy metal against her skin. Stephens shouted 'NO' but it was lost in the roar from the pistol. Barnwell brought the pistol back to bear on Stephens as his body quivered in orgasm inside the dead girl. 'We're not going to have a problem here are we Neal?' he said.
Stephens only shook his head in silence as he watched his partner withdraw from the still body in front of him. Barnwell motioned for Stephens to start filling his Bergen with dollars while he zipped back up his camouflage trousers. 'Get as much as you can, this is going to be a good day.' Stephens was still in shock at seeing the girl murdered in cold blood before his eyes as he stuffed the heavy bag with crisp bank notes from the trapdoor. There were still bundles of the dollars left in the hiding space when Stephens could no longer fit any more in. With the Bergen full of money he watched in astonishment as Barnwell picked a small knife from the bed and stabbed himself in the shoulder with it, letting out a small grunt of pain as he did so. He placed the blade in the dead girls hand and turned to Stephens, 'Self defence, no other choice. Now let's get out of here and stash that cash. We will try and come back for the rest another day.'

Except there was no other day. The suspect they had detained died in captivity while still protesting his innocence and asking about his daughter. Jim Barnwell was implicated in the abuse of Iraqi prisoners but no conviction ever came from the military or civilian justice system and Stephens notice of his promotion and posting to 14 Int came through. He had never told anyone of what happened that day and he came away from Iraq with $250,000 in cool hard currency.

It was while he was over the water in Ireland that Stephens met up with Barnwell again. His techniques for gaining information were put to use in the fight against terrorism and Barnwell enjoyed his job, perhaps a little too much. It was Barnwell that Stephens had stabbed in the pub that day. The barmaid was then stabbed with the same knife by Jim Barnwell because he thought she had been giving information back to her husband. The information was not about British troops or sensitive information, but about the growing drug trade business Barnwell had been building.

Too many of his small time dealers were getting stuffed into backs of cars and kneecapped, or, if it was their second offence, were being found dumped on waste ground with a bullet to the head. Stephens was trying to remove the knife from her body when she died in his arms. Barnwell was too much of an asset to the army in Ireland and so Stephens was made a scapegoat and sent away. Barnwell kept in touch though and every month £10,000 in cash made its way to Stephens. That is the money he used to start his company, Allied Honour Security Systems.

Now Barnwell was back in his life with another money making scheme but this time the figures were astronomical. Millions of pounds were being made and as long as not too many questions were asked, everybody got a share. That was a problem for Barnwell. It was his idea, his scheme. His thoughts were 'Why the fuck should everybody else profit from this…it's mine.'

ONE PIECE AT A TIME

So he employed Stephens to take the other people out of the picture once the plan was almost at fruition. Stephens, on seeing the people he had to deal with, had no qualms in killing them off. Drug dealers, rapists, murderers, terrorist fundamentalists…the world was better off without them in his opinion. It was unfortunate that certain bystanders had to get in the way from time to time, like the police today, but acceptable collateral damage was a military way of life. As long as the job was done and done well, civilian casualties are always acceptable.

Stephens is brought back to the present as Barnwell points to their warehouse just up ahead.
'Did you see that? I think some fucker just went in through that old fire escape.'
'Are you sure?'
'Dunno, I saw something so let's make sure.'
They both hurry towards the warehouse entrance whilst staring at the dark shape of the window above them. Barnwell unlocks the door and enters the porch area.
'Get in…hurry up.' he hisses to Stephens.
Closing the door behind him they are enveloped in the darkness as they shut off the daylight from outside. The big man carefully pushes the door in front of him inwards, wincing in the dark as it scrapes along the floor. Neither of the men move at the sound it makes. It is only when they hear cautious footsteps on the metal stairway that they move forward slowly themselves. The darkness is absolute except for a small beam of light that bobs its way down from the walkway above. Stephens has his hand on the shoulder of the man in front of him as they watch the light reach ground level and move more quickly towards the doorway leading to the back of the warehouse. He squeezes it gently and pushes it forward slightly and they move silently, following the light beam over their own familiar territory.

A rectangle of light appears and they watch a man step inside quickly before the light disappears and they are once again back in darkness.

'You have your gun?' Barnwell whispers back over his shoulder.

'Always.' is Stephens' answer.

They move forward again with more urgency until they reach the closed door.

CHAPTER 42

Luke finds himself inside a brightly lit room and his eyes need a second to adjust to the glare before him. Off to the right he spies a gloomy area lit by dim spotlights that pick out a stained area of floor inside a crude ring and Luke feels a chill shoot down his spine. He walks with wary determination towards the arena he has only seen before on video and scans the corners of the room for cameras. He manages to pick out four that are high up on the walls all pointing their black lenses towards the ring. None of them are showing a red light to indicate they are transmitting or recording any video. Apart from the ring in the centre of the room there is nothing else to indicate the presence of the computer equipment needed to relay the data around the web. Luke knows he should leave straight away and call in the investigation team, but he also knows that time is of the essence. He backs slowly out of the sparse area and resurveys the area.

A pair of doors lay straight ahead and opposite the fighting area is another open entrance to another room which lays in darkness. A camera is placed in the corner of the room to capture the entrance to the fighting room. He pops his head through the squared off entrance and sees racks upon racks of computer equipment all showing their steady green power lights and an occasional flash of amber or red as a hard disk reads information.

'Bingo.' he says out loud as he moves into the room. Luke taps and swipes his finger across the screen of his phone and also takes a few quick photos with the camera function before he runs across the hallway and takes a shot of the ring. He quickly composes a message 'I found it, take a look…get here quick.' and sends the data off to Wilks works mobile number and makes his way back to the doors. Placing his hand on the cold metal he holds his breath as he pushes down the handle and pulls the door open towards him. A similar sized area awaits him through the doors.

A small cupboard stands against one wall next to a heavy looking door that is secured by a deadbolt near the top of the frame. To his left is yet another open area through which he sees something that looks like a walk in freezer you would find in a butcher's shop. It dawns on him what that would be used for and he starts to walk towards it with a morbid sense of dread of what he may find inside but on reaching the door he cannot bring himself to open it.

Leave that to the experts, he thinks as he backs away. His foot bumps something and a metal bucket half full of water crashes over, spilling across the concrete floor with its contents.

'Shit.' he exclaims out loud as he bends over and rights the bucket with a scrape. He looks over his shoulder impulsively as if to see if someone has heard the noise but there is no-one there. His gaze falls upon the deadbolt and the door.

The ringing of his mobile phone startles him so much it slips out of his grasp and smashes into the hard surface of the floor. The protective case splits in two and Luke watches the battery fly out and skid through the water puddle in front of him.

'No answer. Shit!' Wilks turns to me as I drive at full speed through the city streets with sirens and lights blaring and flashing away.

'Try again.' I say, without taking my eyes off the road and the kamikaze pedestrians who are oblivious to the lights and sounds coming from the car. 'If he has just sent those pictures then he must have a signal. Try him again and tell him to get the hell out of there.'

Wilks nods and punches the small screen on the phone with her thumb before bringing it back up to her ear.

'Come on, come on, come on. Answer the phone Luke…just answer the goddamn phone.' She says it like a mantra as the phone rings and rings without being answered.

Luke is looking at the cracked screen of his dripping phone in one hand and the soaking wet battery in the other.

'Shit.' is all he can say as he rubs the battery against his jeans in a bid to dry it off. The casing of the mobile phone is relatively intact but he sees water droplets in the void where the battery should sit and he knows he cannot risk placing it back in without causing possible serious damage to the sensitive electronics.

He looks around for a cloth to wipe it down but sees nothing. Walking to the cupboard he pulls open both of the top drawers not thinking or worrying about leaving his fingerprints at the scene. He smiles slightly as he finds a stack of small cotton bags and pulls one out to dry the battery compartment. Removing the sim card he dries that off first and then turns his attention to the interior of the phone. He wipes the metal contacts of the card slot and then the battery contacts before pushing the cloth into the corners and crannies of the phone.

After a few seconds and satisfied he has done a good enough job he replaces the sim, the battery and pushes the case back together before hitting the power button. As the screen lights up and two hands stretch across the cracked screen to an annoying jingle, Luke breathes a sigh of relief. He puts the phone on the desk while it waits to boot up and get a signal and moves to the bolted door. Placing his ear against the pitted surface he hears nothing from the other side. With his head still firmly pressed against the door he reaches up with one hand and slowly eases the metal rod though the sturdy hoop with a slight grating sound. He takes a step back from the door with an expectation that it will fly open, but it stands impassively before him. His hand stretches out towards the handle and he twists it slowly to open the door.

The ringing phone makes him jump but not as much as the jolt of 50,000 volts that assault his nervous system at the base of his skull. Luke drops to the floor in a crumpled heap before even being able to cry out in pain or fear.

Looking down at the crumpled figure before him Jim Barnwell lets out a small laugh.

'Did you see how that fucker dropped? Jesus that was impressive.' He turns to Stephens who has entered the area just a few steps behind him with his pistol in his hand, 'Do you think he's dead?'

Without waiting to find out he bends down and presses the small metal studs of his tazer against Luke's neck again and presses the trigger. Luke twitches uncontrollably and lets out a groan as his semi-conscious figure is assaulted again.

Again a cruel laugh, 'Look at that. He's pissed himself. I always wondered if that would happen.'

'Stop fucking about. If he has found about us then so have others. Get rid of him and get rid of the girls. I'll destroy the servers, we will just have to make do with the money we have and get out of here before his friends on that phone there turn up. We do this quickly and we do it now, understand?'

Jim nods and stands up. 'Seventeen million is enough for anyone.' he says watching Stephens make his way to the racks of computers. He leans over and touches the still ringing phone with his tazer and has to jerk his hand backwards quickly to avoid the blast of plastic and metal from the exploding device. He pockets the torturous device as he steps over the prone figure and pushes open the door while drawing a large knife from inside his jacket. 'Hey girls, I have a little present for you. I hope y...'
The door is pulled from his grasp as it is yanked inwards and the last thing he sees is a spike of grisly white bone as it punches towards his face. The screams of the girls as they attack him mingle with his own screams as his body is subjected to a vicious hacking, slashing attack. Somewhere in amongst the shouts, shrieks and grunts, Barnwell's last thoughts are that he hears laughing coming from somewhere. A woman's laugh he realises, then he hears no more.

Stephens stands shocked at the carnage in front of him. The soft sucking sounds of the knife as it enters the ripped and tattered carcass are accompanied by a punching sound from the makeshift club in the other womans hands as it smacks into the bloodied face of his now ex-partner. As he watches the man die on the floor he feels a brief sense of satisfaction, which is quickly replaced by self preservation. Forgetting the servers and the destruction of their data he runs from the room and the warehouse. He is not even noticed by the two women as they continue to pummel the body they are kneeling over.

CHAPTER 43

I skid to a halt in front of the warehouse building and don't even bother to switch off the engine before I am out of the car and running for the door. I hear Wilks screaming at me to stop but I ignore her as I push through the partly open door, through a small, covered and blacked-out porch and into a large dark area. The only point of reference is a rectangle of light at the far end of the building and I move forward quickly to reach it. I catch my breath in the darkness before entering the doorway. Standing to one side of the door frame I glance quickly into the space beyond. I see an open clear area and a door that is standing slightly ajar. I push the door open slowly as caution overtakes the adrenaline coursing through my body and I understand how the commissioner may have found himself in just such a situation. I hear low sobbing coming from the room ahead and my heart skips a beat…Helen.
I rush through the room and burst through the door frantically staggering backwards in shock as I try to make sense of the vision of hell before me. I recognise Luke lying motionless on the floor off to the left. A woman is standing over him and staring down at him. She is wearing what looks to be a thin, gossamer, clinging, red dress and she is holding a strange looking club. Another figure is making small movements over a bundle of rags and unrecognizable lumps just in front of an open doorway.

The light spills through into the room beyond and I can make out the pale flesh of at least one and possibly two dead women. It is difficult to tell at this distance. The woman standing over Luke starts to raise her arms as if to bring the club down on his still form. My mind suddenly makes a connection as her arms reach their zenith and I see she is not wearing a dress but is covered in thick streams of blood from head to toe. Her arms are now fully stretched out and her hair is swept back by their upward movement to reveal a snarling face, her lips stretched wide in a terrifying grimace.
'Helen,' I shout, 'Helen, stop. It's Peter. Helen…NO'
Her arms swing down but as they do so she jerks her head up to look at me. The weapon in her hands crashes down onto the floor inches from Luke's head as my sister stares at me with features I barely recognise so contorted is her face. I see her face soften as she looks into my eyes and the recognition hits her. Her head drops to the item she holds in her hands and she flings it away with a heart wrenching cry. I expect her to collapse as I see her legs buckle slightly but she moves to her left and squats down next to the other woman and wraps her in her arms.
'Zoe…Zoe…it's over. We're alive. You're alive.'
I stand and watch as my sister and the other woman wrap their arms around each other and cry uncontrollably together as they are surrounded by blood and intestines and other unidentifiable parts of a dismembered body. I turn away and throw up against the wall, the bitter taste in my mouth is sweeter than the stench coming from the room. I feel a hand on my shoulder and Wilks is there saying things I do not hear as I look back to my sister and Zoe entwined together in the blood of their kidnapper.
'Helen.' I mumble.
A pair of wide eyes look up at me as I say her name. I swear I see pure hatred glare out before she drops her gaze back to the blood covered woman she is holding.

One hour later I am standing at the side of a hospital bed as Luke is being checked out for any injuries. Helen and Zoe would not be separated even to get into an ambulance. I wanted to go with them, go with Helen and be with her but she just kept shaking her head and repeating 'No'. The two of them are in a secure room further down the hall being assessed by medical staff and treated for their physical injuries. I am sure their psychological wounds will take much longer to heal.

'What's the prognosis, Doc?' JD's voice breaks the silence as he enters the room and clasps me on the shoulder.

'Well, he's a very lucky man. There are superficial contact burns on the back of his neck with associated bruising around the area. The bruising on his forehead here,' a gloved hand points to the left side of Luke's forehead, 'this was a worry. We thought there may be some concussion or other damage from the fall to floor, but it appears your friend here has a very thick skull.'

JD smiles, 'Which is what got him into this trouble in the first place.'

'Yes well,' the Dr continues, 'I would like to keep him in for few hours to ensure he has no latent injuries from the shock or the bump to his head and then he will be allowed home.'

'Thanks Doc,' I say, 'it's much appreciated.'

The Dr gathers his clipboard and strolls away whilst making notes.

'I messed up didn't I?' Luke, looking up to JD and myself says with a quiver in his voice.

JD removes his hand from my shoulder and places it on Luke's arm.

'If you call going in half-cocked, unprepared, with no idea what you might find while rescuing two kidnapped women from certain death at the hands of a crazed killer messing up…then yeah, you messed up. But I have to tell you that you did some great work today. Two women are still alive because of you, Helen Carter and Zoe Walker are both in this hospital being treated because you took a risk.'
JD grips his shoulder a little tighter, 'I for one would like to thank you for what you call your mess up, and I know two families who would like to do the same.' He turns to me.
I nod and repeat the words I have been saying all morning.
'I can't find the words to say, Luke. Thank you seems so inadequate for saving my sister's life.'
'Did you see what happened?' Luke asks.
'It was all over by the time I got there.' I say shaking my head, 'The Ripper who has yet to be formally identified as James Barnwell was dead and you were out cold when I entered the room. At least you stopped him somehow and we hope to get the full story when Helen and Zoe are able to talk.'
'That's not what I mean,' Luke replies. 'Before I was knocked out I used my phone to link into the local server and start the cameras to relay the feed and location back to the lab.'
'Like you did in the office with the US assault feed.' I say with a hint of awe in my voice.
'Pretty much the same sort of thing, yeah. The whole thing will be recorded on the hard drive of my computer at work.'
JD and I stare at each other and then both turn to the young man as he starts talking again.
'Let's make sure the right guy was involved shall we? I'll sign myself out and we'll check the recording at the lab.'
He looks at the two of us as we stare at him open mouthed.
'What?' he says.

Fifteen minutes later, after giving the Dr full assurances that Luke will not be left alone for any time over the next 24 hours, we are able to leave the hospital. I am driving with JD in the front seat and Luke sitting in the back. JD relates the information from the explosion earlier.

'It looks like the Commissioner somehow got hold of some information about the warehouse being used to hold the kidnapped women, which we now know to be false information.' He glances over his shoulder at Luke, 'It was actually being used to securely route data from the dark web for the Ripper's video streams as well as other more traditional criminal activities. The man who rented the building, a Bosnian by the name of Dvorin Milicevic, has been under our observation for a while for suspected human trafficking, prostitution and under age sexual activities. The bastard was supplying young Bosnian and Serbian girls for use all around Europe with London as one of his main bases. We think he may have been in the warehouse at the time of the explosion and there is no one on the force who is mourning his loss. Ten bodies have been removed from the rubble, the commissioner has been identified along with the members of the ARU. We suspect the others to be Milicevic and members of his gang.'

'What caused the explosion? Any clues on that front?' I ask.

'We have traces of PE4 explosives at the scene…those EOD guys are fast workers with their sniffer kit. Apparently PE4 is a slightly different version of C4 plastic explosive but only the UK and French military use it. That's the good news as it means it should be traceable within the military circles it's used in. The bad news is that the French have "lost" a whole load of it during their operations in West Africa and maybe that is how the Bosnians got a hold of it.'

'So a dead end there.' I pause as I navigate through the traffic that surrounds us, 'What about the computer equipment, is any of it salvageable?'

ONE PIECE AT A TIME

JD looks straight ahead as I swerve around a bike messenger who is attempting to become the latest statistic on the London roads.

'Too early to tell. We'll need our wonder boy here to take a look at it with his team when the site is cleared.'

Luke leans forward, 'As long as the drives are not too badly damaged we should be able to gain some information from them.'

'Good.' I say.

The car goes silent which is not what I want. I am trying not to think of Helen and the look on her face as I entered the room. I am scared of the psychological damage that has been caused by her terrifying ordeal.

'Luke tell me how you knew where to go today. How the hell did you manage to locate that warehouse amongst the 100's that are out there?'

As Luke explains his software program and the almost imperceptible repeat of data streams, IP and MAC addresses, I try to concentrate on his words to ward off my thoughts. It doesn't work and my mind keeps drifting back to my sister and how I fear that even though she is alive, I have lost her for good this time.

As I pull into the secure car park I notice the media have already made their camp at the front of the building.

'News travels fast it seems.' I say.

JD shrugs his shoulders, 'The biggest news story and man hunt this century *and* a police commissioner being killed on duty is sure to get the creative juices flowing. I just hope they give the families some respect and stay away.'

We exit the car and make our way to the bland concrete façade.

'Peter.' A female voice cries out from the side gate.

I look over and see Ann Clarke standing there.

'Peter, this is not about the story. I just want to say I am thankful your sister is OK. How are you? How is she?'

I pause, looking at her with confused feelings running through me.

'JD, Luke, go on ahead I will be in a moment.'

'She's still the press Peter, be careful.' JD announces with caution as he moves away and into the building.

The pedestrian entrance is barred and locked by a blue metal gate but Ann reaches through as I walk over to her and grasps my hand.

'I have been so worried for you..and for Helen,' she adds almost as an afterthought, 'I just wanted to…oh I don't know, I just wanted to make sure you were alright after the explosion today. I didn't want it to be you.'

I notice tears glistening in her eyes as she stands there holding my hand through the bars.

'Peter, I know we have had our differences and I know you say it can't work but I am different now. I thought I had lost you and that made me think how good we were together.'

She stares at me with her wet eyes, 'We were good together weren't we Peter?'

The question catches me off guard and I nod slowly. 'Yes…yes we were…but..'

She smiles at me and reaches her other hand through the bars to hold mine, 'Don't say any more Peter, not yet. I still have feelings for you Peter, strong feelings, and it is only after thinking you were dead that I realised just how strong they are. Peter, I love you, I want you back in my life…I know it's the wrong time with so much going on with your investigation, but I needed you to know how I feel and I hope you feel the same way too.'

She has a desperate look in her eyes as she seeks my reassurance. I have already seen the hurt I have caused in one person I love today and I cannot bring myself to hurt anybody else. I nod,

'I have to go, Ann. We will have to talk later.'

I release her hands and walk away but not before seeing a look of relief cross her face. My thoughts are even more troubled as I enter the building, heading after JD and Luke.

CHAPTER 44

It only takes a few minutes of Luke tapping away at his keyboard to bring up the video feed recorded from the warehouse earlier.

'Why did you do it? Why did you set the cameras going?' JD queries.

'I thought it was the easiest way to send the location through to HQ and ensure we were getting the clear data, you know, non encrypted. If you look here,' he smudges a fingerprint across the screen at a list of IP addresses, 'it also gave us a clear stream of information on the locations and MAC addresses of the PCs that have been accessing this information. I thought it might be useful in the investigation and for creating warrants for at least a search of premises which correspond to these IP addresses.'

I rub my eyes only understanding half of what Luke is saying.

'There you are.' JD points out as on the screen Luke walks into shot.

We watch as he walks over to the desk and search it in an attempt to find something to dry off his phone. Luke looks embarrassed,

'I dropped it in a puddle of water.' he says.

As his attention is taken up by the phone and then on the locked door in front of him we see two men walk in from the bottom of the screen. Just as Luke opens the door the larger of the two presses something against Luke's neck and he drops to the floor. When the man turns around and says something we see it is Jim Barnwell, immediately recognizable from the photofit images produced by Stephens. The other man still has his back to the camera.

'There are two of them in on this. Who's the other guy?' JD wonders aloud.

ONE PIECE AT A TIME

At that moment the door is yanked inwards catching Barnwell off balance and we see how he is attacked by Helen and Zoe. 'Jesus.' Both Luke and JD exclaim at the same time as they watch the violence inflicted upon the screen.

I am watching the man at the bottom of the screen and see him freeze in horror, just as I did. Then he turns and for a brief moment I get a look at his face before he rapidly moves out of view.

'Stephens, the other man involved is Neal Stephens. He was stringing us along all the bloody time.' I shout out to the room. 'Pause the tape, rewind it a few seconds.'

Luke does as I ask.

'There, stop it. Can you zoom in and print that out.' I say. Luke moves his mouse in small movements across the desk until we have a grainy, zoomed in picture of Neal Stephens on the screen.

'It's not brilliant,' Luke says, 'but that's down to the resolution of the camera. I'm sorry but it's the best I can do, it's not like you see on the TV.'

I point at the screen, 'I want that son of a bitch found. Send copies of that photo to everyone.'

I pull my phone out and call Wilks.

'Ma'am, we have another suspect in the case. It appears Barnwell was not working alone, there's another man involved.'

The answer from my boss almost knocks the wind out of me, 'You mean Neal Stephens. I already know. Graham is here with me telling me his findings from yesterday.'

'What...how...? We have only just found out...'

'Come up to my office with your information while Graham is still here. We will go through it all together.'

She hangs up as I stand there wondering how Graham worked it out. I grab a copy of the printout of Neal Stephens from the printer tray.

'Both of you come with me. The super already knows about Stephens so we are one step behind again.'

Graham is sitting opposite Wilks at her desk and they are in mid conversation when we walk in. She stops talking to Graham and directs her attention to us instead.

'Come in gentlemen, sit down. It looks like the investigation has come to a conclusion with this evidence. Dr Young, would you like to do the honours.'

Graham stands up and motions for us to sit down as he walks over to the window and opens it.

'Oh sorry, Patricia, may I?' he points to the opening. 'I need some air.' She nods her approval.

'James Barnwell and Neal Stephens have been linked in the kidnapping and murders of the women involved in this case. We have no definite visual identification from the two surviving victims because either they were always hooded and blindfolded or the men entering the room and who abused them in the building were always wearing masks also. The building is part of the disused chemical works that was purchased by Allied Honour Security Systems. This company is headed by a man we know as Neal Stephens, an ex- Royal Military Policeman.

We can confirm Barnwell was found dead at the scene today by dental records and I will soon be getting a match back from the DNA profilers. It's lucky that all military personnel have to give a DNA sample before going to a conflict zone to aid identification if the worst happens. The army have been extremely swift in providing the information regarding Barnwell.' He pauses and picks up a sheet of paper from Wilks' desk.

'This is the DNA report from the lab about our murder victim the other day and the hair found in the box with the severed hand. They match and conclusively show that Neal Stephens is our victim. It also shows that DNA collected from his body can be traced back to Barnwell and two other sources. We are waiting to confirm but we believe it is from Helen and Zoe, the two girls rescued today.'

'Hold on Graham,' I say, 'if the dead body the other day that you have matched is Neal Stephens, then who is this guy who gave evidence last week under that same name?'
I wave the picture in front of me, 'This…this is the Neal Stephens we know. He is the other man we are looking for and he was alive today just before I entered the warehouse. This picture is from a recorded video feed started by Luke here when he entered the building.'
I place the print out on the desk in front of the superintendent and Graham who now looks as confused as the rest of us.
'If this is not Stephens,' I stab at the picture with my hand, 'then who is he and why has he taken Stephens name?'
The ringing of the phone on the desk interrupts me. Wilks answers it.
'Yes, Superintendent Wilks…who?...Here in this building?...Put them in interview room number 1, keep a guard on the door and we'll be right down.'
She looks around the room at us all,
'A man saying his name is Neal Stephens has just entered reception with his lawyer asking to speak to the officer in charge of the Ripper investigation.'

CHAPTER 45

We have all moved quickly down to the observation area for interview room one. The large one way mirror shows two men calmly sitting at the metal table not saying a word to one another. The man I recognise as Neal Stephens holds his wrist up to take a look at his watch and slowly turns his head to face the mirror. He cracks a smile as if he knows we are there and then turns back to face his companion.
'I know that guy.' says Luke pointing at the glass.
'Of course you do, that's Stephens.' retorts JD.
Luke twists his head from the window to look at us.
'I mean the other guy. He's not a lawyer but something to do with military intelligence, SIS. He came to me when it was first discovered I had hacked into, shall we say, sensitive areas. He tried to recruit me into his department. To be honest he scared the crap out of me and he couldn't, or wouldn't answer any of my questions, so I said no. Two days later I am being interviewed by Superintendent Wilks here and being threatened with a jail term or university. She was…I mean is, much nicer.'
'Flattery is a thin compliment Luke, but I will take it.' Wilks says smiling, 'Why didn't you mention him in your interview with me?'
'I didn't really have him on my mind when you were explaining my options. At least you gave me options, he was just full of threats and warnings…and I believed him.'
I started walking towards the door.
'Peter.' Wilks' tone makes me stop.
'Peter. Watch your step with this one. JD go in with him. Say nothing and watch the SIS chap. I have a bad feeling about this situation.'
JD steps towards the door next to me.
'Ready?' he asks.

'Let's see what he has to say.' is my reply.
I enter the interview room with JD right behind me.

We walk in and sit down opposite the two men with our backs to the mirror. JD leans over to start the recording device, 'DCI Peter Carter and DI John Dawkins. Interview room one, date…'
'I'd prefer if you didn't do that detective.' The so-called lawyer says.
'Why is that Mr…?' I ask.
'Mr Carter, I will only have to remove the tape and all video evidence of our presence here anyway. Also as my companion has not been charged with any crime I would assume this is an informal interview and has no requirement for being recorded in such a manner. Why waste another government asset. Hmmm?'
I nod towards JD who turns off the equipment.
'Do you mind telling us who you are,' I look from the intelligence man to Stephens, 'who you both are.'
The smile he gives me makes my blood boil and I have to tell myself to calm down.
'Our names are not important. What you should be asking yourself is why we are here. We have much to offer you for your investigation but you will have to cooperate with us.'
I cannot believe my ears,
'You want *us* to cooperate with *you*. What on Earth are you talking about? You are in my interview room, under my jurisdiction and in my control until I say otherwise. You want to be charged? I will start with kidnapping, trafficking, rape, money laundering and to top it off the murder of eight innocent women and six police officers. How does that sound for cooperation to you?'

The SIS man leans forward and folds his hands on the desk. 'And just what evidence do you have for any of those charges Mr Carter? DNA? Fingerprints? I'm not sure there is any way you could get a warrant for arrest without evidence. Suspicion…we both know that being suspicious of someone does not make arrests stick.'

He sits back in his chair. 'You have nothing…but we can offer you answers. Would you like answers, Mr Carter?'

I clench my fists together under the table as I try to keep a check on my anger. This guy knows we have very little and is taunting us…taunting me.

The door to the interview room is pushed open and Wilks walks in brandishing the printout from the video feed.

'We have a photo of your man at the scene of a crime, brandishing a firearm. I say we could charge him with illegal possession and obstructing the course of justice to begin with. You know, that last charge would apply to you too unless you tell us who you are and why you are here. I don't give a crap about your SIS 'need to know' shit. This is my turf and you are stuck here until I say you can go. All I have to do is mention terrorism and we have you for a minimum of 72 hours before we even have to inform your bosses at the big building.'

'Ah, superintendent Wilks, how nice to see you. You could of course do that but you know it would be pointless and you would all be kissing your careers goodbye. Look we came here to assist your investigation, not be given empty threats and…'

'Six police officers, one of which was the Commissioner of the London Metropolitan police force have been killed. I will not let those murders go unpunished and your friend here is implicated in all of this.' Wilks manages to force these words out through her clenched teeth.

'A very unfortunate incident, one that should never have occurred and you have our sympathy. But I believe your forensics team will find that the place was rigged to blow if discovered or threatened. The Bosnians are a strange lot, they would rather die than see their partners in crime convicted by association so they exploded their device to save their friends. Your officers were in the wrong place at the wrong time. I have it on very good authority that there would have been a military raid on the warehouse a few hours later, probably with a similar outcome. But we in the military can face acceptable losses for the greater good.'

Wilks does not move as she hears his words.

'You knew about the explosives.' her voice is just above a whisper, 'You knew and didn't see it fit to inform my department to warn my officers of the danger. You could have saved lives.'

'As I said Superintendent, acceptable losses are at the heart of any operation. The Bosnian we wanted in that building, a man called Milicevic, was deemed to be an excessive risk to the interests of this nation. It was an operation sanctioned from the very top of our government, your officers jumped the gun and it went wrong. You were to be informed one hour before the assault to remove your officers from the area and reduce the threat of casualties. To be frank, we don't know how your commissioner managed to be there with an armed response unit in the first place. Heads will roll because of that I assure you. We will find out where the leak came from and deal with the problem in our own way.'

I have been watching Stephens throughout this exchange. He has remained impassive, almost bored, in his chair.

'Why were you at the warehouse with James Barnwell? What did you have to do with the kidnapping of the girls and their murders? If you are not Neal Stephens, then who are you?' I ask my questions quietly and deliberately, directing them across the table to him.

'You say you came to help this investigation, then help us. Give us some help as to what we are actually dealing with here. It's obvious it is more than just a killer or you wouldn't be here.'

He looks across to the man next to him. I see the faintest of nods and then he starts talking.

CHAPTER 46

'My name is Neal Stephens and most of what you have been told about me is correct. I was RMP before joining an intelligence unit and meeting Ree...' he catches himself in time, 'meeting my friend here. I deal mainly with tracking down and infiltrating organisations that are less than friendly to our democratic way of life. We used to be able to track and trace e-mails, websites and electronic communications with a fair amount of ease, but that has all changed over the last year or two. Security systems have been made that make tracking any form of electronic messaging extremely difficult but my team and I have so far, in conjunction with the Americans, managed to crack them all. Then TOR came along.' He sighs. 'Nothing we have managed over the last twelve months has even come close to breaking the trail of a single e-mail message. TOR is so effective at what it does that we fail every time we try. The Americans are scared shitless of it, they see millions in e-currency pass though it hourly and there is nothing we can do about it. The worst thing is that it is free and everyone has access to it. I mean everyone.

Kids are passing their dad's porn across it or sharing pictures of themselves with wolves on the net. Nothing we can do. Paedophiles use it to swap god-knows what, nothing we can do. Our agencies are worried because we have seen a huge drop in traffic that we normally are able to pick up and this is information we need to stop the next 9/11 or 7/7. TOR is a terrorists and organised crimes dream come true. It was my job to try and infiltrate the network by any means possible to track these guys down. You may have heard of Allied Honour Security Systems, a company set up in my name. We provide equipment which is used throughout the world for physical security. All, and I mean all of the equipment supplied by that company comes from the intelligence services, whether it be MI6, the CIA or Mossad. We now share our information like never before with cooperation that has not been seen since the Second World War and we have been getting results. My problem is that certain groups have been getting suspicious. Well laid plans are going wrong, it is not a coincidence that there have been no spectacular events for a while but rather small splinter groups that do their own thing. Anyway, a price has been placed on my head. A big price and so I have to disappear as Neal Stephens. A man was murdered two days ago by Barnwell. This man was his partner in the making of the videos that were streamed online. His name is, or was, Carl Metters. I don't believe he knew about the girls being murdered, he was told by Barnwell that they were all street girls who would do anything for money, including getting beat up. That was Barnwell's pleasure, hitting women. Barnwell and Metters got into an argument somehow and by the time I arrived Metters was already dead. I saw my opportunity and said I would dispose of the body. We are pretty similar in appearance so it wouldn't be too difficult. My companions simply swapped my records for that of Metters and that is that.'
He sees my look as I open my mouth.
'Did you know about the killing of the women?' I ask.

He says nothing but nods his head in the affirmative.

'You let women be killed and you allowed it.' I slam my hands down on the table making him jump. 'What kind of a man are you? Why didn't you inform us so we could do something about it?'

He sighs, 'When I found out what was happening to the women it was already too late. If you remember I came in and informed you of Barnwell's appearance that night. I was hoping he could be stopped while our mission continued without him. I never expected Metters to be killed or for your investigation to run so slowly.'

'Your records that were left here?' I ask.

'Again, doctored quickly to give you just enough information to give me credibility and make you take me seriously. It was touch and go about that phase of the operation. Some people thought we shouldn't release Barnwell's information to you, they thought it might jeopardise the operation. But the two of us, we fought that decision. We couldn't let more women be killed.'

I shake my head as I look at him.

'But the abuse and the rapes were OK? Torture, kidnap, violent sexual abuse in front of cameras is fine, but hey, look at us we tried to stop them being killed. Jesus!' The last word explodes from mouth.

'Mr Carter,' the other man starts talking, 'there is more at stake here than the lives of a few unfortunate women.'

I stand threateningly, 'One of those unfortunate women is my sister.' I growl.

'That may be the case, but we are talking about the possibility of saving hundreds if not thousands of lives in the long term. You must understand it is just a matter of figures and percentages for us. We are not, must not, be personally involved.'

As I launch myself across the table at him JD springs up and restrains me.

'Don't Peter…don't give the slimy bastard the satisfaction,' he says directly into my ear.
I straighten my jacket and slowly sit back down, glaring at him. To his credit the other man did not even flinch.
'It is personal feelings that cause trouble in our line of work. We must remain focussed and detached from the matters we deal with or mistakes are made. I believe that is what happened with your police commissioner. Personal feelings got in the way and he made a mistake.'
This time Wilks moves forward and no-one is there to restrain her. She slaps him sharply across the face as tears spring to her eyes.
'You should have told us.' she says.
'No time dear, no time. The first we knew was when Stephens here was waiting for the military team to enter and saw your officers enter the building. What could we do?'
Stephens butts in, 'If we had known there was a police operation going on at the warehouse we would have shared the information about the explosives, but information is a two-way thing. We knew nothing, so we could do nothing. I am sorry for the losses to your officers but it was your Commissioner's actions that decided their fate.'
Wilks says nothing and we all realise he is telling the truth.
'The operation with Barnwell, what could he have to do with terrorist organisations?'
Stephens lets out a soft chuckle as if I have said something amusing, 'He was using TOR to buy and sell drugs. When he came up with the idea to stream videos around the network he had so many contacts within the TOR community it was unbelievable. Many terrorist and criminal organisations use drugs and prostitution to fund their activities, Barnwell was a lynch pin in the whole system. He was moving millions around the globe from the Middle East to Russia, the States to China, you name it he had contacts. He had been under surveillance for a while but we needed a man on the inside and I was the logical choice.

It was thought that with our security devices installed into his servers, which I supplied, we would start to be able to trace the data flow to and fro. Once we managed that, our tech guys said it would be easier to start decrypting the messages themselves, and we would be back in business beating up the bad guys. That didn't happen. We were getting nowhere and we came close to shutting down the whole thing. I mean removing Barnwell from the picture and replacing him with one of ours, someone like me. Then information started coming in during your operation that your team were making breakthroughs with TOR traceability and that focussed our thoughts again. We would let you guys break TOR and use your information to crack down on groups we were after. Your first intelligence provided definite information on a Pakistani fundamentalist group which the Americans were very grateful for. A sequence of events started from the information found on their servers that has involved operations in Israel and a viable threat assessment of an imminent attack on a sporting event somewhere in the US. It is hoped that the increase in security will reap the benefits and thwart the attack before it begins and it is all down to you guys. You have already saved hundreds of lives without even knowing it.'

'So you were stringing us along the whole time. Letting us sweat as we struggled with our investigation.' I comment.

Stephens shakes his head, 'It's not like that. I would not have let anything happen to the two remaining girls, your sister and that other one. If they had not attacked Barnwell I would have disposed of him before he had a chance to do anything and you would have received a tip off to check out the building. By then of course you would have my DNA with a murder victim from two days ago, Barnwell dead and we would have ensured there was enough evidence linking the two to close your case.'

His friend talks over Stephens,

'That is still the case. If it wasn't for that picture you would not even know about us. The reason we came down here today was to fill in the missing details for you and ask for your cooperation.'

'That cooperation word again. All I can think of doing is charging both of you with obstruction of a police investigation and holding you until I can find something else to pin on you.' I spit out.

'Without that picture you have nothing. Look Peter, may I call you Peter? All we want is the software that you have used to break the TOR algorithm. The threat to national…international security is far beyond your comprehension. We would like your cooperation but we don't need it. We want to show how we are not the bad guys here as long as you help us. All you need to do is close the case, celebrate the victory and there is no need to make any mention of us. You walk away with your head held high knowing you have done all you can and helped your country to maintain its interests both domestic and foreign.'

I look at Wilks and see the resigned look on her face. She knows we are beat and I feel the same way. JD places his hand on my shoulder, he doesn't have to say a word, we all know it is over. They have us over a barrel and they know it.

The man from MI6 sees our look and smiles,

'Just give us what we need or…' He checks his watch, 'I can have my team here in ten minutes with authorisation to remove that data and any other data from your servers as we see fit. I don't want to do it that way, I prefer to make friends and then keep them on my side. You help us,' he turns to Wilks, 'we help you. Isn't that how it works? We all need a little help and loyalty now and again and remember we need a new commissioner now. I have the ears of some very important people who make such decisions.' He turns back to me. 'Loyalty is everything don't you think?'

I want to smack his grin from here to the MI6 building but I know he has won and even though the satisfaction of beating him would be great, it won't help me.

'This isn't over.' I say as I stand and walk towards the door, towards my office, towards Helen, towards Julia and towards my life
I don't turn around or even pause as he calls after me,
'Oh but it is, old chap. It is.'

Printed in Great
Britain
by Amazon